WHO FRAMED KLARIS CLIFF?

nikki sheehan

OXFORD
UNIVERSITY PRESS

OXFORD
UNIVERSITY PRESS

Great Clarendon Street, Oxford OX2 6DP
Oxford University Press is a department of the University of Oxford.
It furthers the University's objective of excellence in research, scholarship,
and education by publishing worldwide in

Oxford   New York

Auckland   Cape Town   Dar es Salaam   Hong Kong   Karachi
Kuala Lumpur   Madrid   Melbourne   Mexico City   Nairobi
New Delhi   Shanghai   Taipei   Toronto

With offices in

Argentina   Austria   Brazil   Chile   Czech Republic   France   Greece
Guatemala   Hungary   Italy   Japan   Poland   Portugal   Singapore
South Korea   Switzerland   Thailand   Turkey   Ukraine   Vietnam

Oxford is a registered trade mark of Oxford University Press
in the UK and in certain other countries

British Library Cataloguing in Publication Data
Data available

ISBN: 978-0-19-273572-0
1 3 5 7 9 10 8 6 4 2

Printed in Great Britain
Paper used in the production of this book is a natural,
recyclable product made from wood grown in sustainable forests.
The manufacturing process conforms to the environmental
regulations of the country of origin.

For Eira, wherever you are

Contents

A Small Hand

We were talking about the old days, and I remembered the weirdest things. Like people calling them 'friends'. And how they said they were good for your brain. Some families even laid a place for them at dinner.

Then I thought about the day it changed. The day Shorefield happened.

It was on TV. A newsflash cut through the kids' programmes. We saw the victims being rolled out on trolleys, their faces covered over. A camera zoomed in on a small hand dangling from underneath a sheet.

The next day they put on a special assembly at school and the kids who had them were taken into another room.

The headmaster told the rest of us that we should never play make-believe games by ourselves, because that's how it happens.

That's how they get in.

MONDAY

Ear Hair

I took a deep breath and banged the side of my head hard against the wall.

It hurt like hell.

'Now just go away!' I hissed.

'What are you doing, Joseph?' my dad called from the hallway. 'Did you fall out of bed?'

'No, just trying to kill something.'

He appeared in the doorway. It was early but he was already dressed and smelling of mint.

'Hmm, a horsefly was it? There was one in the kitchen last night. Nasty little blighters. Anyway, I've done you an egg, sunny side up, and two slices of granary. We should be OK if we leave by half past. The appointment's not till ten.'

'What appointment?'

'The optician. I reminded you yesterday.'

I groaned. I'd planned to see Rocky. 'Does it have to be today?'

My dad grew a few more wrinkles as he thought, which is pretty nice for an adult. Most of them just expect you to do the old they-say-jump-you-ask-how-high.

I grabbed my dressing gown and headed down the creaking cottage stairs. Dad followed and pulled up a chair, waiting until I'd nearly finished eating before he started on about it again.

'Well, I could cancel your test, I expect. But I'd like to go for mine.'

He touched the strip of Elastoplast that had held his glasses together for ages. I thought he hadn't bought new ones because he doesn't like changing things. Things like his 1987 canary-yellow Ford Capri ('She's a classic, Joseph'), or his ageing-rock-star haircut ('People have mistaken me for Jon Bon Jovi'). Or the relationship status on his Facebook page ('She might just walk back in one day. You never know').

'I have to get back to work next week, and no one'll want me to fix their plumbing looking like this,' he said. 'The thing is I was hoping you'd help me choose—they might not do this style any more.' He took the glasses off, held them close to his face, and squinted. 'Your mum chose these; she seemed to know what suited my face. I haven't got a clue. And don't say a paper bag.'

While he talked, my eyes settled on the last postcard, propped up on the bookshelf behind him. It had arrived a couple of years ago, the day before I turned eleven.

But it didn't say happy birthday son, or sorry for not sending a present. It said she'd be back in the summer.

My dad was waiting for an answer. Of course I should go. He'd taken the whole school holidays off work to be with me. But it was the end of August and the gluey back-to-school feeling in my stomach was getting harder to ignore. A day of mindless fun was just what I needed, and Rocky was the master of mindless.

Besides, Klaris usually left me alone when I was with him.

'Sorry, Dad. I said I'd hang out next door today. Can't you ask someone who works there to help you choose?'

He smiled at me, but it was the sort of smile he does to stop me feeling bad, which made it even worse. In the background Klaris was trying to say something. I would've put my hands over my ears but I knew it didn't help, so I pressed my teeth together hard to stop myself from shouting at her. My dad must've noticed my strange expression because he put his strong-skinny arm around me and pulled me close.

'It's all right, Joseph, no need to get upset. You're thirteen now. I understand you've got your own plans. I'm big and ugly enough to go to town by myself.'

I finished up the last crust. 'Thanks, Dad, that was great. I'd better get dressed.'

He took the plate from me and plunged it into the

washing-up bowl, then stared through the window into the back garden. 'That bindweed's getting hold again.' I followed his gaze and saw a trail of white flowers, like bells, smothering a bush. 'I told your mum to dig it up from the roots when it first appeared, but she wouldn't listen. She said it was pretty.'

He rinsed the plate and put it on the drainer before turning to me. 'You would tell me, Joseph, wouldn't you, if something was wrong?'

I shrugged. 'Nothing's wrong.'

'It's just that the teenage years can be confusing.' He looked thoughtful. 'So can your early forties come to that. Anyway, I just wanted to say that you can talk to me about anything.'

I looked up.

Was this it?

Was this the moment I'd been waiting for, when I could finally tell him about Klaris? I wanted to, or I thought I did. But how could I say it without making him as scared as I was?

Dad turned to face me, grinning. 'Anything at all: girl trouble, body changes, bad taste in music, all that teenage stuff. Whatever it is, Joseph, I bet I've been through it too.'

Bet you haven't, I thought.

Out loud I said. 'Don't worry, Dad. There's nothing wrong. But if you've got anything you want to talk to *me* about: ear hair, forgetfulness, dodgy fashion sense. Y'know, all that middle-aged stuff.'

He smiled, but I think he knew I was bluffing him. 'No. I'm fine too.'

And I wondered how much longer I could keep her hidden.

The Final Bend

We've always had an open-door thing going on between the Cliff family's house, Potter's Lodge, and our humble abode, Kiln Cottage, which is attached to it like a big pink boil on its bum.

So, as usual, I walked across the half-bald shared lawn, kicking the puffy white head off a dandelion as I passed, and went straight in through their back door.

It was dark and quiet inside, and with five kids, two dogs, and the normal number of parents living there, that was unusual. But I knew exactly where I'd find Rocky.

In the living room the red velvet curtains were closed but I could just about see him sprawled on the rug in front of the TV. His body was limp, dressed in his summer-holiday uniform of combats and camo T-shirt, and his new number one haircut was so short his hair was like iron filings clinging magnetically to his skull. He looked like a corpse really, apart from his hands, which were alive and well and gripping the PlayStation controller.

He crashed, swore, and looked up.

'Wassup, Joseph? Wanna race?'

My hands twitched and I obeyed. 'OK.'

I can never resist driving games. I always beat Rocky, I always beat everyone, and I know it's stupid, but I love winning, even against someone who plays like a blind man in boxing gloves.

'Choose your weapon then.'

I picked up a controller and went for my favourite car, the green one with the white stripe across the bonnet.

He groaned. 'Aw, c'mon Joseph, not that one. You know you'll win anyway. Lemme have the best car.'

'It's not the vehicle, y'know. It's what you do with it that counts. Have a motorbike. They're faster.'

'So how come you want the car? Tell you what, you can have it as long as you play left-handed.'

I smiled. 'OK.'

The thing is I'm pretty good left-handed. All those evenings, waiting for mum to come back, I practised with both hands. I even tried it with my feet, and I could still just about get round the track.

We lined up. I flexed my fingers till the knuckles popped, and brushed the hair out of my eyes—I'm good, but I still need to see.

Then it was 3-2-1 and we were off.

Anything could happen while I'm playing—someone could come in, take my trainers off, cut my toenails and paint them pink, and I wouldn't notice. At first it was the usual story. I felt like I really was driving the impossible car, not sitting in the crumbs and dog hair on the Cliffs' saggy sofa. But then, as I approached the finishing line, coming up through the noise and the adrenalin, getting louder and stronger with every second—

Her.

Klaris.

It felt like she was shouting. But somehow I knew she wasn't angry—she was excited. Really excited.

'Shut up!' I muttered, keeping my voice below the roar of the game. She went quiet for a few seconds, but as I drove round the final bend I knew she was still there, and I had that feeling you get when someone stands too close and you have to breathe in what they breathe out.

Then she started cheering, and I lost it. I was seconds from the finishing line but I stood up and hurled the controller across the room at the armchair. It bounced off and hit the floor, the back and the battery flying in opposite directions.

Rocky stared at me, open-mouthed. 'What d'you do that for? You were gonna win.'

'I just . . .' I could feel sweat on my upper lip.

'Y'alright, mate? You look a bit weird.'

'Yeah, just feeling sick. It's stuffy in here.' I went to the curtains, pulled them open, and heaved up the bottom sash of the window. I breathed in deeply then spoke to the air in a thin whisper. 'Happy now? Is that what you wanted? Why don't you just go back to Flea and stop ruining my life!'

Posh Tea

When I turned round Rocky was kneeling with his head under the sofa groping for the battery. His trousers had slipped right down and his big white behind was mooning at me, which didn't help my nausea much.

He emerged with a red football sock covered in fluff, a pound coin, and, what he'd been looking for, the vital silver-grey battery. He shoved the sock back under, pocketed the coin, slotted the battery into the controller and switched on.

'Yay, still working. Come on, one more round. You left-handed, me with the green car, and the loser has to do a forfeit—winner's choice.'

I laughed. Rocky's not really stupid, but he's definitely too optimistic for his own good.

So I played again, and won—smashed him actually—and Klaris left me alone.

While I was winning I felt normal, like nothing was

going on. Afterwards I just did the usual victory dance around Rocky's living room, and reminded him of the loser's forfeit.

'I think I'll go for a ...' I grinned in what I hoped was a crazy-axe-murderer kind of way. 'A number seven. You have to drink a cup of tea sieved through my sock.'

'You're joking, Joseph. That's sick.'

I grinned. 'Actually, you invented seven yourself. I thought you'd want to be the first to try it out.' I threw the controller, more gently this time, onto the sofa. 'Go and put the kettle on.'

The Cliffs' kitchen is so old fashioned that it looks like the Victorian Home exhibit at our local museum.

Instead of a cooker they have a rusty old green range with a clothes dryer full of underwear hanging over it. Then there's the mismatched wooden cupboards and big old pine table in the middle. Where we have lino on the floor, they have flagstones that are uneven with big cracks between them, and every time one of the Cliffs drops a glass it smashes into a million pieces and someone shouts, 'Sack the juggler,' which stopped being funny ages ago.

Rocky had his hand in the pig biscuit barrel that used to oink, and was groping around, the tip of his tongue poking from the corner of his mouth. 'Oh, come on, you beauty. Yesss!' He pulled out an ancient-looking chocolate digestive, so covered in biscuit dust that its shiny brown coating had been camouflaged. He broke it in half and gave me the larger piece.

'Thanks,' I said. 'But don't think you can bribe your way out of the punishment.' I slipped off my trainer, followed by the grey sports sock that had once been white, and dangled it in his face. It still held the ghostly shape of my foot, but with a coin-sized hole in the big toe.

Rocky wrinkled his nose. 'When was the last time you changed these?'

'Clean on this week.' I paused. 'Or last.'

'I know, how about a rematch?' he tried. 'Loser has to do *two* forfeits.'

I laughed. 'Get on with it. It's just a slightly damp, very smelly sock. You know you've done worse.'

Rocky frowned. 'Yeah, but never to you. Only to Flea, and that doesn't count.' He sighed. 'All right, but just one sip. I'm not drinking the whole thing.'

I shook my head. 'Under the rules of engagement you have to either do the punishment yourself, and that means drinking the whole lot, or find someone else to do it for you, and there isn't anyone else. So you'd better get on with it.'

There was silence for a moment as Rocky shovelled spoonfuls of his mum's lapsang souchong tea leaves down into the foot of my sock. When a trail started to pour, like ants, from the toe he put it into a mug and filled it to the brim with hot water.

'This posh tea'll disguise the taste,' he said. 'D'you think I should have it with milk? My mum likes it black.'

'Definitely a splash,' I said. 'Milk and cheese go together well. They're practically the same stuff.'

He dunked it for a bit, then slopped the tea-filled sock into the sink and reached for the sugar. 'This is gonna need a lot of sweetening.'

'Hey, don't take all the sugar,' Pooh said, coming into the room clutching a vampire novel. 'I want a cup of tea too.'

I'd noticed that she was now about an inch taller than me, even though I'm a few months older. She was wearing denim shorts and a white vest top, and the weeks spent lying in the garden had turned her skin brown and bleached her long hair to a pale straw colour.

She sniffed at Rocky's tea. 'That smells nice, kind of smoky. Think I'll have one of them too.'

'You don't usually drink this fancy stuff,' said Rocky. Then he whispered loudly to me, 'She's trying to look mature to impress you.'

'Dream on,' said Pooh, but her cheeks went pink. 'Move out of the way so I can make myself one.'

Rocky grinned at me and held his cup out. 'Here you go, Pooh, I'll let you have mine. I think I prefer the normal stuff.'

She took the cup from him, giving it another sniff.

'What've you done to it?'

Rocky frowned. 'What d'you mean?' He put on a sort of abandoned puppy face. 'You think I've poisoned it, don't you? Oh my God, Pooh, you're unbelievable! I do something nice for you, my only sister, and you think I'm trying to kill you. It's s'posed to smell like that. It's posh tea. Posh tea always smells funny. That's the point of it. Come on, Joseph,' he said, standing stiffly, 'Let's leave Pooh to enjoy her "poisoned" tea.'

As we left the room she must have noticed the sock in the sink.

'Hey, what's this?'

We ran out to the garden and lay on the grass laughing. I took off my other sock and hid it in my pocket.

'Don't worry, Joseph,' said Rocky. 'If she realizes I'll say Klaris did it.'

My heart did a sort of bunny hop. 'Yeah, but Flea's not here,' I replied, trying to sound normal. 'So how could it have anything to do with Klaris?'

Rocky grinned, his large front teeth reflecting the sunlight. 'Haven't you heard? Klaris has been a naughty little imaginary person. My dad thinks she's going rogue.'

I tried to control my voice, but couldn't trust myself to say more than, 'Why?'

'Oh, it's just a load of little things, but Dad keeps saying that's how it started at Shorefield. Y'know, one minute they're hiding the toothpicks, and then before you know it they're murdering us all in our beds.'

He started ripping the petals off a daisy. 'Wouldn't have thought little Klaris would have it in her, personally. Anyway, he's talking about calling in the Council.'

'What, you mean for the Cosh?'

He nodded. 'Yeah, but I don't reckon he'll do it. Not to Flea. He's all talk.'

I tried to digest this information for a moment, but it gave me a stomach ache. I hadn't told anyone that Klaris was bothering me. I couldn't. It's only weird, loner kids like Flea that have imaginary people in their heads. Not thirteen-year-olds with mates, who play in a football team and aren't particularly good at art or writing, and definitely don't have an over-developed imagination. Not kids like me, who are so normal it's almost *ab*normal.

And no one, no matter how abnormal, has someone else's. Not unless they've migrated that is, which wasn't something I was ready to think about.

'So, what's she supposed to have done?'

'Oh, nothing much. Dad's just annoyed cos she's been turning the lights on in the car and running the battery down so he has to walk to work. You know how lazy he is.'

'Just the car lights?' I asked, when all I really wanted to know was, is she driving anyone else mad by invading their head and taking over their thoughts?

15

'Dunno. Ask crazy boy,' Rocky nodded his head towards Flea, who was walking across the lawn on his tiptoes smiling, but not at us.

'Oi, Flea!' shouted Rocky. 'Joseph wants to know what Klaris has been up to.'

Flea gazed in my direction for a moment, his eyes blank and his mouth gaping like a fish on ice, then he turned and ran back to the house.

'How rude,' said Rocky. 'That boy needs to learn some manners. Not surprising no one likes him.'

But I knew he wasn't being rude. He was listening to Klaris. And he didn't like what he heard.

Like a Goldfish

My dad was back from town and reading the paper.

'All right, sunshine? Ready for some lunch? There's tomato soup boiling on the hob. Help yourself.'

'Thanks.'

The thick, red-orange liquid hissed at me as I poured it into a bowl.

'I miss Mum's cooking, Dad.'

'Yeah, me too, son. Specially her fry-ups in bed on Sunday mornings.'

I dropped the pan into the washing-up bowl where it gave up with a sigh.

'I don't remember that.'

He looked bewildered for a moment, and his eyes, a greenish brown, not boring blue like mine and Mum's, stared at a spot just past my ear. 'Oh, p'raps that was before you were born. I'm losing track now.'

'I remember her lasagne though, Dad, and her roasts. They were the best.'

He frowned. 'Hey, watch what you're saying, you cheeky tyke. Claire's a wonderful woman, but her roasts were never a patch on mine. Her veg was crunchy, her gravy was lumpy, and her Yorkshire puddings never rose. You and me used to call them UFOs—Unidentified Food Objects.'

He folded the paper and smiled.

'Course, I taught her how to do them, in the end . . .' His smile faded.

I looked over at the postcard. 'What do they eat for Sunday dinner in Spain, Dad?'

'Dunno. Paella?'

'Can we have paella this weekend? I'll find a recipe on the Internet.'

'Yeah, if you like. I could show you my bullfighting techniques too, while we're at it.' He jumped up, grabbed a red tea towel and started flapping it to one side. 'Torro! Torro!'

'Yeah, right.' I turned back to my soup.

'What? There's a lot of things about me you don't know, Joseph.'

'Yeah, and the fact that you're a champion bullfighter isn't one of them.'

He smiled. 'P'raps not. But there's time, I'm still young.'

The soup was searing hot. While I waited for it

to cool I cut my bread into little squares. I launched them into the bowl like spongy rafts, and stirred the soup round and round until they starting swirling. I imagined that the centre was a sinkhole and they were going to be sucked down.

Then I realized what I was doing. Thirteen years old and still playing games like that. No wonder Klaris got in. I must've practically left out a welcome mat.

'Anyway,' my dad tried to smooth the twisted seam of the tea towel. 'I wanted to talk to you about something.'

'What? Middle-age spread and girlfriend problems again?'

'Well, sort of. I was thinking of going out later in the week. On a kind of . . .' his voice dipped. 'Date.'

'A date?'

'Well, it's just a drink with someone. A lady.'

'A lady? A date with a lady? You?' I studied his face to see if he was joking. 'Are you sure?'

'Yes, Joseph, of course I'm sure. Anyway, what's so surprising about that?'

'Nothing. I suppose.'

'So, anyway, she's just someone I met through a forum online. It's nothing to get overexcited about. But I wanted to ask you what you think. If you mind.'

I thought about it. Of course I minded. Had he forgotten he was still married to Mum, even if no one knew where she was?

I shrugged. 'It's not really up to me, is it?'

'No, but . . . Well, it's just a vague plan and she might change her mind, once she's seen me in the flesh. But if I do go maybe you can stay next door for the night.' He sighed and folded the tea towel. 'Anyway, paella on Sunday. Definitely. Only do we have to have all the shellfish in it?'

'Yeah, I want it to be authentic. But you can pick yours out and I'll eat them if you want.'

'Joseph, you do know paella has squid in it too?'

'Squid? You mean, like octopus?' He nodded and I shuddered. 'Well, maybe it doesn't have to be completely authentic.'

I took a sip of soup. It made my tongue tingle like a painful version of sherbet. I wanted to talk to him about more than paella, but I didn't know where to start.

I took a deep breath.

'Dad, did you know that Klaris has been causing trouble?'

'Flea's Klaris?'

'Yeah. Rocky says his dad's going to get rid of her.'

He hung the tea towel up on a peg and exhaled loudly. 'Things must've got worse.'

'What d'you mean worse? Has she done something before?'

My dad shifted his weight and dropped his voice. 'Well, there was the incident with the rabbit.'

'I thought that was the dogs.'

'Yes, but I know Klaris was blamed for some reason. Anyway, it's very sad. For Flea, I mean.'

'I don't think anyone else will miss her much. I reckon they'll throw a party when she goes.'

He shook his head. 'I wouldn't wish the Cosh on anyone.'

I looked up from my soup. 'Yeah, but they're pests, aren't they? And if she's out of control someone needs to do something.' I tried to read his expression. 'Don't they?'

'Well, I know all that. But she's important to young Flea. And what they have to do to get 'em out . . .' My dad looked towards the open back door then back at me. 'I'm not sure it's right, that's all I'm saying. Not unless it's a life and death situation.'

'You mean like Shorefield?'

He paused. 'Yeah. Like Shorefield.'

He watched as I wiped up the final smears with the surviving raft, but then dropped it back into the bowl. I wasn't hungry any more.

'Course, it was different when I was young, Joseph. There wasn't this fear of them. And they didn't have the Cosh then.'

'So how did they get rid of imaginary people?'

'They just went when they were ready. Kids grew out of them, like milk teeth.'

He paused. 'There was one occasion that I know

about though. He had no brothers or sisters, this kid, and Velvet, the imaginary person, was probably his only mate. Anyway, I'm sure his mum and dad thought they were doing the best thing. They didn't want anyone picking on him at school, calling him a weirdo, you know what kids are like.'

I did.

'So they decided that Velvet had to go.'

'Yeah, and what did they do?'

My dad smiled. 'They flushed him down the toilet.'

'Down the toilet? Like a goldfish? Oh, come on, Dad. Stop winding me up.'

He shook his head. 'I'm not. They took the boy into the bathroom. Then he had to say goodbye to Velvet and get him to jump in the toilet. When he'd done that they flushed.'

'And did it work?'

'What do you think?'

'Well, I don't know.'

'No, neither did they. But the boy said he'd gone, and there was no more trouble from him, so everyone was happy. End of story.'

I looked at my dad grinning like an idiot. Sometimes I wonder about him.

'So are you saying the imaginary person didn't go?'

'No, I'm saying that everyone was happy. Isn't that the most we can hope for, son? A happy ending?'

A happy ending. I couldn't imagine it. I felt like we'd been trapped in the sad middle part for two years.

I started wiping the sides of my bowl again, going round and round, until it was spotless.

'Dad, what happens if imaginary people migrate? Does everyone they've gone into have to get coshed?'

'God, the questions you ask, Joseph.' He thought for a moment, his brow crinkling into ridges, like new Plasticine. 'As far as I know it's like rats. You have to block off anywhere they might run to.'

He ruffled my hair. 'Anyway, that's not something you need to think about. The migrating comes way down the line, so you're not going to catch anything from hanging round next door.'

And then, right on cue, Klaris interrupted my thoughts, buzzing at me like a mosquito. If I could've coshed her myself I would cheerfully have done it.

I turned away from my dad so he couldn't see the look on my face, mumbled, 'Going out,' and walked over to the back door.

Safe—for the Moment

I stood resting against the door frame, looking over the lawn. It was a mess. There was a three-wheeled skateboard and quite a few faded blue crisp packets poking, like weeds, up through the yellow grass. Cheese 'n' onion. I knew they would be Rocky's; he's the only person who can stand them.

I could also just make out an old model plane, army green, half melted out of shape. The plastic had dripped into lethal spikes that you don't see when you're walking barefoot—that had to be the twins. I don't know if they hid them in the long grass on purpose, but they were spread out like land mines, and, after you'd trodden on one or two, you started to wonder.

Closer to the Cliffs' house was Pooh's striped sun lounger. Not officially hers, but no one would risk climbing onto it. It was much safer to lie on the lawn and get bitten by ants.

There was nothing to show that Flea lived there. Not unless you counted Klaris, hanging around me, flicking the flies and wasps away when they flew too close.

I suppose if I'd been watching Klaris protecting Flea like that I would've laughed. It was like she was playing insect tennis, vibrating the air molecules to ping the confused bugs away when they came within a few inches. But I was terrified that someone would find out, and anything she did, especially something so obvious, made me furious.

'Just get lost, won't you? I don't need your help.'

She must've gone then because the air around me sort of thinned, and a huge horsefly landed on my leg.

I brushed it off then looked over to the fields beyond the garden that lead to Goat Island. Compared with the scruffy lawn they were neat, like a yellow blanket. The corn was waist-high, but I knew that soon the whole lot would be hacked down to grey stubble, leaving the view towards the Island ugly and empty.

And then the wind would come whistling over the field, and the summer would be finished. Another summer gone. Another summer without my mum.

I missed her all year round, of course I did. But with the end of the sunshine I stopped hoping. I didn't hold my breath as I walked in from school, willing her to be sitting by the fire reading, or cooking my dinner, or laughing at something on the TV.

Or staring out of the window hugging her knees, crying silently.

But when my birthday came close I started to believe that she'd turn up some time soon. Because in her last postcard she'd said she would be back in the summer. She'd promised. So I knew she would. It was just that she didn't say which summer.

Flea appeared like a ghost at the open window next door. If I had to describe him I'd say he had wispy no-colour hair and a pale complexion with big grey eyes and blond eyelashes. I'd probably also say he had a slight build, with pipe-cleaner-thin arms and legs, and his clothes always looked like they belonged to someone else.

The frown on Flea's face as he looked over at me was definitely his own. I was pretty sure now that he knew about Klaris and me, and he didn't like it one bit. So I was surprised when he disappeared from the window, came out through the back door, and walked over.

I tried to act normal. 'Hi, Flea. What's up?'

He looked down at the dry ground in front of him, breathing deeply. Thankfully, I couldn't hear her, but I knew the signs. He was struggling with something Klaris was saying.

'D'you wanna tell her to shut up a minute so you can think?'

He looked relieved as Klaris, evidently, shut up.

'Thanks. That's better,' he said. 'She's a bit agitated

at the moment because of everything that's going on.'
I sighed. I wasn't sure I wanted to have a conversation
about Klaris. But I certainly didn't want to have a conversation about her that could be overheard by my dad or
anyone else. So I walked over to the middle of the lawn,
with Flea following, and stopped by the old dry bird bath.

'So, what is it, Flea?'

'I just want you to promise you're not going to tell
anyone.'

'Tell anyone what? Oh, on second thoughts, just
forget it. I don't really want to know.' I turned to go
back to my house.

'She's desperate for you to understand. She won't
stop talking about you and the picnic and—'

'What picnic? I don't know what you're on about,
Flea.'

'She says you're not listening, and you've got to.
She's really upset and she's worried that if they get rid
of her—'

'This is crazy, Flea! It's got nothing to do with me.
You wanna have someone living in your brain? Go
right ahead. But *I* don't. So you can both go away and
leave me alone!'

I never usually shout. The Cliff lot shout all the time
and no one would even notice one of them yelling. But
I hardly even recognized the sound that had forced its
way out of my throat. But what had I said? Had I given
anything away? I was about to find out.

'Oi, Flea, stop being weird and freaking Joseph out.' Rocky to the rescue. He had climbed through his living room window into the weedy flowerbed, and was ambling over, still clutching the games controller. He reached us and draped his arm around my shoulder, glaring at his little brother.

'Just ignore him, Joseph. Don't let him drag you into his strange world.'

I could breathe again. I'd given nothing away. No one knew about the gatecrasher in my head except me and Flea. And maybe Flea doubted it now. I was safe—for the moment.

Vulpes Vulpes

Back inside the house my dad was at the computer talking and laughing on Skype with a woman I didn't recognize.

I flopped onto the sofa and listened to him trying to be charming for a while. But I couldn't relax, and not just because of his awful flirting. I'd remembered that it was the last week of the school holidays and I hadn't even started my summer project.

So I dragged myself off the sofa and found the library book that I'd brought home in July—*Vulpes Vulpes: the Indigenous British Fox*—and started work.

I copied out some boring stuff about habitat and diet, but if I wanted to impress my new teacher I needed something unique. So I searched through a few crammed cupboards until I found the camera.

We had hardly used it since Mum went. She was the family photographer. Me and Dad tend to cut people's heads off, so we haven't got many photos with her in. Well, not from the shoulders up.

The light was fading as I slipped into the garden and ran down to the apple tree at the end.

Climbing it wasn't as easy as it used to be, especially with the hard-backed book in one hand, and the camera slung around my neck. My old foot holes had suddenly shrunk into toe holes, the branch I settled on bowed and creaked, and the ridged bark dug hard into my bum.

I didn't have to wait long for some action down below, but it was just Flea's mum calling her lot in for dinner. She's got this thing about having the whole family at the table for meals. We used to do that too. It's funny that you can miss things you never even knew you had.

After that it went quiet again, and I spent ten or fifteen minutes peering into the dusk, squinting every time I thought I'd glimpsed something, but it was always just out of sight, or in my imagination, I wasn't sure which. Then I was distracted by shapes moving behind the Cliffs' kitchen window, and I heard chairs scraping and cutlery and plates clanging. There were footsteps, and I saw the twins come out into the garden.

The thing with Wills and Egg is that they look very sweet. Their big brown eyes are round like an animal's, and, though they're five, their almost black hair has never been cut and it reaches down to their trousers. People often mistake them for girls because they're beautiful, like children in an oil painting.

From my perch I could hear them talking, but their words sort of flow like music, with no breaks in between, and not even their mum can understand their private conversations. But I could tell that one of them had something secret in his pocket.

They were just a few metres from my tree when Flea appeared in the doorway. Wills and Egg paused and looked at him for a second, then turned and walked away. It was impossible to tell which twin had decided to break the moment and move first; it was like they were one person with two bodies. Flea stayed where he was, staring into the dark of the garden for at least a minute before walking over to the middle of the lawn and lying down on his back, his legs and arms outstretched like he was making a snow angel.

While I'd been watching Flea the twins had disappeared from sight. I wondered if they had gone back inside, maybe through the front door. But then I heard them again, the low purr of their voices blended into one tone, and the odd higher, excited notes, coming from the shed end of the garden.

I'd had enough and started to climb down the tree but, because I couldn't see what I was doing, I slipped and grated my palms on the rough bark. Crouching low in the shadow of the bushes, swearing silently, I tried to brush the dirt out of my hands.

It was dark now and most of the windows of the big house were glowing. I gazed over towards my cottage, hoping it would look cosy, but our poky, deep-set windows were dark. Dad was probably still at the computer and hadn't noticed the time. I wanted to run for home, flick on the lights and wash the bark and moss out of my stinging hands, but I hesitated because, just at that moment I heard a scraping sound and the Cliffs' bathroom window rattled open. A face, older, but with the same dark hair as Rocky and the twins appeared, framed in steam.

'Egg! Wills! Are you out there?' It was their mum. The twins came strolling out of the shadows and walked slowly towards the house, as if going in had been their idea in the first place.

But Mrs Cliff stayed at the window. In the gloom I could see a yellow spark, followed by a pinpoint orange glow from her cigarette, which lengthened as she inhaled.

'She likes to smoke in secret. She thinks we don't know she's doing it.' The small voice came from the middle of the lawn. His head turned towards me. 'Did you see any foxes, Joseph?'

'God, Flea, you nearly gave me a heart attack. What are you doing, anyway?'

'The same as you. Just enjoying nature.'

I stood and brushed myself down, trying to pretend that I hadn't been lurking under a bush.

'I don't think enjoying is the right word. Anyway, how did you know what I was doing?'

'I saw the book: *Vulpes Vulpes.*' He flipped over onto his front, propping himself up on his elbows. 'You missed it.' He looked over to the bushes beyond the house. 'It's not really your fault. You have to know where to look.'

'What are you talking about?'

'The big fox. It comes up by the side of the house cos that's where the bins are.'

It was annoying that Flea knew where to look and I didn't, but I realized that he could help me. 'D'you think it'll come back?'

'Perhaps, if we wait quietly.' Flea took half a bread roll from his pocket. 'This might help too.'

He threw it across the grass a few metres from where he was lying. We waited in silence for what felt like hours until, at last, I saw a shadow move across the lawn. I got the camera ready, but the fox took its time, strolling slowly up to the bread as if it dined there every day. It sniffed the roll, swallowed it down whole, then looked over at Flea for more. I was so stunned I forgot why I was there until Flea glared at me. I aimed the camera and pushed the button. The click and the flash startled the fox and it disappeared back into the night.

'Got ya! Thanks for that, Flea.'

He beamed as he got up and walked over to me. 'That's all right.'

There was a moment's awkward silence. Me and Flea weren't what you'd call friends. The conversation earlier was probably the longest we'd ever had, and that hadn't exactly gone well.

'I'd better head back,' I said. 'My dad'll be wondering where I am.'

I turned to leave, but he gripped my arm.

'No. Wait a minute.' The smile had gone, and was replaced by a look of desperation that was plain wrong on a seven-year-old. 'I've helped you, Joseph. Now it's your turn to help me.'

A catch—I should've known.

He produced a tightly folded piece of paper from his pocket.

'It's the list. The list of stuff my dad thinks she's done.' He unfolded the paper and held it up. 'He says if she does one more thing he's sending it straight to the Council. You're going to help me prove she's innocent.'

Klaris was back in my head telling me to agree. I didn't want to argue with her in front of Flea, so I just said, 'I can't even read it. It's too dark now.'

'OK, we'll look at it together in the morning.' He gave me an awkward hug which I didn't return. 'I'm so relieved. She said you'd help, but I wasn't sure.'

34

'Look, Flea, I, er . . .' But he wasn't listening.

'Meet me on the bench in the morning, nine o'clock.' And he was gone.

Back at home the only sound was Dad tapping at the computer in the living room. I washed most of the dried blood from my hands then sat at the kitchen table, polished off a packet of custard creams, and, without disturbing him, went to bed.

That night I dreamt I was inside a volcano. It was as hot as hell and so dark that I couldn't see myself. Somehow I knew my mum was trapped in the magma chamber below me and it was down to me to rescue her. I started picking up boulders, even though the skin on my hands was already blistered and bleeding, and I hurled them behind me like they were made of polystyrene.

Then I felt the volcano vibrate and everything shook so hard my teeth rattled. Balls of red-hot magma started whizzing around, lighting up the dark, splatting and sizzling on the sides of the chamber, and then, from nowhere, a massive rock smashed into me.

I woke up and touched my forehead. It hurt. But how could I get injured in a dream? I checked again. There was a little dent just above my eyebrow. As I turned on the bedside lamp I felt the shaking again, but this time I knew I wasn't dreaming. It was actually happening.

The whole room was vibrating and I could hear a low rumble like the engine of a truck.

As I looked towards the door I saw two fine lines zigzag their way through the plaster around the frame and I began to yell. 'Dad! Dad! The house is falling down!'

TUESDAY

The Dent in my Forehead

'Stars shinin' bright above you
Night breezes seem to whisper
I love you
Birds singin' in the sycamore tree
Dream a little dream of me-ee—Ow! Damn!'

That was the sound of my dad shaving. The internal walls of Kiln Cottage are really thin and the bathroom's next to my room. I can hear everything he does in there; the tap running to wet his toothbrush, the bristles scrubbing away at his teeth, which, incidentally, lasts about ten seconds, not the two minutes he always tells me to brush for. Then the tap's on again and there's a clink as he puts his toothbrush back in the cup. Next I hear him gargling and spitting out his revolting green mouthwash.

Unfortunately, I can also hear him use the toilet. Every detail.

You can tell a lot about someone's state of mind through a bathroom wall. In the early days, after Mum didn't come back, I used to hear him crying in there. He would lock the door too. He told me that I should cry if I wanted to, but he was ashamed of his own tears.

'Sweet dreams till sunbeams find you
Sweet dreams that leave all worries behind you
But in your dreams whatever they be
Dream a little dream of me.'

I put the pillow over my head and the singing stopped. Through one eye I could just see my dad's face, scrubbed and scraped pink, and with a patch of tissue on his chin.

'Good morning, sunshine. Glad you had a bit of a lie in after last night.'

He ran his fingers over the network of cracks around the door. 'Yep, I'll get a bit of filler today to fix this. Could've been worse though—4.8 on the Richter scale! Imagine that. On the news they're saying the epicentre was Dudley Zoo. Those poor animals. Must've thrown the penguins into a panic, eh? It's scary enough for us, and at least we understand about seismology—well, the basics anyway.'

He pulled open the curtains.

'I'm gutted I missed it actually. Can't believe I slept

through the whole thing. Your mum always said I'd sleep through an earthquake. Looks like she was right. Again. Still, they're warning there might be an aftershock, so hopefully I won't miss that.'

He sat on the edge of the bed, reached down and picked up a book. 'What's this? *Vulpes Vulpes*?'

'Oh, that explains it,' I took the pillow off my head and lifted my fringe to show him the dent in my forehead. 'I'd left it up on the shelf. Must've fallen off in the earthquake.' I rubbed the mark gently. 'I dreamt that a big rock hit me.'

My dad felt the sharp corners of the book and drew in a breath. 'Weird things, dreams. Some people think they mean something, but I think they're more to do with indigestion. Eat cheese before bed, did you?'

'No. Just half a packet of custard creams.'

He smiled. 'That'll be it then. Your custard cream is more of a tea-time biscuit. It'll be the richness of the filling that did it. Next time stick to something plainer. Anyway, I came to say how about town later? You need a haircut, so we could make a day of it. Go for pizza after. What d'you think?'

I lay back on the pillow again. 'Yeah, sounds good.'

It did. So why did I have the feeling I was being bought?

'The thing is, remember I said I might be going out with a lady friend? Well, it looks like it's pretty definite for Friday, so I thought p'raps you could help me find something new to wear?'

I threw back the duvet and reached for my dressing gown, wrapping it around myself tightly. I was glad of the warmth even though it stopped a couple of inches above my knees.

'So, are you going to tell me who she is?'

'Yeah, yeah, of course. Her name's Mandy. She's a plumber.' I must have looked surprised. 'What's wrong with that? There are lots of lady plumbers actually. You'd like her. Great sense of humour.'

'Yeah, must have to be going out with you.'

'Oi!' He pretended to be hurt. 'Anyway, like I said, it's nothing serious. We just share an interest in the issues facing modern heating and sanitation specialists.'

I sniggered. 'Like what? Backache and the price of pipes?'

He did that superior look he tries sometimes. 'You wouldn't understand.' Then he noticed my hands. 'Oh, my God, Joseph, what have you done?'

'It's nothing. Just a scrape from climbing a tree.'

'Let's have a look. They'll need cleaning out.'

He was reaching towards me.

'No. It's fine. I gave them a good wash last night. But you could make me some eggy bread if you like. I don't think I could cook with my hands like this.'

'Yeah, course. Eggy bread, two slices, coming straight up.'

But he hovered in the doorway for a moment.

'Joseph, me going on a date doesn't mean I'm not happy here, just the two of us. And I'm not looking for a replacement for your mum either. Just the odd night out, that's all.'

'I know, Dad. It's . . . it's fine.'

A Typed List

I walked out into the garden, my second spongy slice of eggy bread drooping in my hand. Flea was already sitting on the old green bench, swinging his legs.

'How's the cicatrization going, Joseph?'

'Eh?'

'The healing process. That's the medical term for it.'

'Oh.' I wondered how Flea could know so much when he'd only had seven years to learn it. 'Yeah, fine I suppose.' There was an awkward silence. 'Well, you'd better show me what you've got, but that doesn't mean I'm going to help you.'

He swung his legs again for a moment, and I could see him struggling with the Klaris noise in his head. Then he held out a piece of paper.

It was a typed list.

Klaris — Misdemeanours

1. Habitually turns on car lights and
   flats the battery
2. Vandalized my stethoscope
3. Killed the rabbit
4. Gave the dogs my whisky (the good
   stuff)

I read the list and handed it back to Flea.

'Not exactly crimes of the century, are they? Nothing that would make you think she's about to go crazy ape and start a killing spree. Look, I don't think you've got anything to worry about. Your dad'll get over it in a few days. Meanwhile you'll just have to tell Klaris to lie low and behave herself.'

His bottom lip trembled. 'Anyone can see she didn't do it—any of it. She couldn't have. She can only use her vibrations to affect the molecules in liquids and gases. She can't even lift the skin off custard. I know because she tried once. But she'd need muscles to be able to unscrew the cap off the whisky or break a stethoscope.'

'But some rogues can use solid objects,' I said, 'Like the knife that killed everyone at Shorefield.'

Flea shuddered. 'That was never actually proved. Anyway, this is just an excuse cos my dad's paranoid about imaginary people. And if he even thinks she's done one more thing he'll phone RIPS straight away—'

'What's RIPS?'

'The Rogue Imaginary Persons Section at the Council—and he'll send them this list. I don't care what they do to me, but they'll kill her, Joseph. You have to help me prove that she's innocent.'

'Even if I wanted to—and I'm not sure I do—what could I do about it?'

'You could be like a detective. Interview everyone and ask questions and find out who really did all the stuff. Then we'd give the evidence to my dad and he'd have to forget all about it.'

I stuffed the last bit of eggy bread into my mouth, and wiped my lips.

'Why don't *you* do it?'

There was silence for a moment. Then he turned to me, and his grey eyes were shining.

'You know I can't. You know they wouldn't listen to me. But they'd tell you the truth. Everyone likes you. No one likes me.'

I was about to tell him to stop feeling sorry for himself, when I saw the fat tears start to slide, reflecting coloured light like opals, and I stopped myself. Mum used to cry like that. Silently, so you wouldn't even know she was doing it. I'd nearly forgotten.

Flea wiped the tears away with the hem of his T-shirt and whispered, 'I don't know what I'd do without Klaris.' Then he looked me in the eye and spoke in a more normal tone. 'She said you'd help. She was sure you would.'

Rocky appeared at the other end of the garden. It was time to finish the conversation.

'Sorry, Flea. Gotta go.'

I walked away.

It was a Joke

I met Rocky halfway across the lawn.

'Hey, Joseph, where are you going?'

'Nowhere.' I didn't want to stop and talk. I felt churned up inside after my conversation with Flea, and that tear thing he'd done, and I didn't trust myself not to say something stupid. So I walked straight past Rocky to the end of the garden and out through the wooden gate into the cornfields.

Rocky, of course, didn't get the hint, and followed me, shouting, 'What are you doing hanging out with weird boy again?'

I slowed down and sighed loudly. 'I wasn't hanging out. We're neighbours. We share a garden, remember?'

'Yeah, but he told me you two were having a secret meeting this morning.'

'So?' I said. 'You jealous?'

'No, course not. But you've gotta admit, hanging around with Flea's a bit . . .'

I stopped walking and turned on him. 'A bit what, Rocky? A bit sad cos his only friend lives in his brain—is that what you mean? Or is it cos he's upset that she's going to be coshed? Is that what's so pathetic?'

Rocky stepped back. 'No, I didn't mean that.'

'OK then, what did you mean?'

He folded his arms and scowled. 'Nothing.'

I turned away and carried on walking, and he followed. 'It's just that it's Flea, isn't it? *Flea!* You know he's a freak, Joseph. Even he'd admit that. In fact I reckon he's proud of it. He doesn't even try to be normal. And it's embarrassing being related to someone like that. You're an only child—you don't know what it's like having brothers and sisters to humiliate you.'

'Yeah, thanks for reminding me.'

'It's not just about Klaris, you know. I s'pose Flea can't help that.' He went silent for a moment. 'Anyway, if you think about it he's pretty lucky.'

I laughed. 'Lucky? What are you on about? He's an outcast even in his own family, and the one person he has in the entire world is about to be killed.'

'Yeah, yeah, I know all that. What I meant is that he's actually quite lucky having a friend no one else can see.'

I stopped. 'Rocky, what are you talking about?'

'No, I've been thinking, you and me, we're best mates

47

obviously. We're always together. But then you have to go home for dinner, and bed and stuff.'

'Yeah, and?'

'But with imaginary people the party never ends.'

I started walking away.

He followed. 'No, really, I'm being serious. I know everyone says they can be dangerous, but I've got that worked out too.'

I stopped again. 'OK, I have to hear this.'

'Well, have you noticed they only tell you stuff's dangerous when it's really good fun? Like knives, and cider, and going swimming at night—all too "dangerous" for us, according to them. Well, what if it's the same with Klaris and her mates? Probably perfectly safe, but the adults just don't want us to enjoy ourselves.'

I was staring at him, trying to work out if he was being serious.

He carried on. 'Think about it. You could have sleepovers every single night. Stay up till four o'clock in the morning. Even school nights. And no one could stop you.'

I smiled. 'Yeah, and they wouldn't eat half the crisps and sweets.'

'Exactly.' He grinned. 'And they could help you cheat in tests at school. It'd be cool.'

'Yeah, but only if you had a boy,' I added, still thinking he was joking.

'Course. And he'd have to be tough. Not a wimp like Klaris.'

'And you'd have to make sure no one knew. You wouldn't want to lose all your real mates.'

'Obviously. I'm not stupid, am I?'

I didn't answer.

He was looking really excited. 'So, how d'you think you get one?'

'Why are you asking me?'

'Just thought you might know.'

I tried to sound casual. 'Yeah, well, as it happens, I might.' Even as I said it I knew I was making a huge mistake, but I couldn't stop myself. At least I had the sense to ask for an insurance policy. 'But you'll have to swear to secrecy.'

He made a sign of the cross over his heart, and we both cupped our left hands and spat in them. Then we shook on it, and he licked his palm.

'OK, so are you gonna tell me?'

I took a deep breath. 'Well, the thing is I don't actually know. But there is someone who does.'

'No,' he said. 'You can't get anyone else involved.'

'It's not a person. It's . . . it's Klaris. I'm going to ask Klaris for you.'

'Still no, Joseph. Cos you'd have to tell Flea, and someone else is bound to find out.'

'You don't understand, Rocky. I can ask Klaris *directly*.'

49

He stared at me 'What d'you mean directly? No one can speak to her except Flea.'

I took a deep breath. 'I can ask Klaris directly because she, er . . .' He was looking confused. 'She talks to me.' I avoided his eyes as I carried on. 'She's been doing it for months. I didn't want her to. I try and ignore her mostly. I'm always telling her to go away. But, if you want, as a favour, I could ask her for you.'

His expression was sort of blank, his jaw hanging.

'What's wrong?' I asked.

He swallowed and spoke quietly. 'That's not the same.' Then he looked me in the eye, his voice hard and urgent. 'She belongs to Flea, Joseph. If she's talking to you she must be migrating. It's one of the stages, you know that. It means my dad's right after all—she's going rogue. Rogues can hurt us, kill us even. Like at Shorefield, and that other place a few months ago. The whole family could be dead by the end of the week. We've got to tell someone before something terrible happens.'

'No, you've got it all wrong,' I shouted. 'She's not dangerous, she's just annoying. And look, I'm still just me. I'm not different, am I? Do I look different? Have I been acting weird? No, course not. I'm the same old Joseph.'

He was staring at me, his eyes fixed on my face like he didn't recognize me any more. Like I wasn't me any more. Like I had finally revealed myself to him. Which, I suppose, I had.

I needed to backtrack fast. 'Please, Rocky, don't tell anyone. You promised you wouldn't. You crossed your heart and we shook on it. Look,' I held up my palm, still shiny from his spit.

I could see him hesitate then. 'You can't break a cross your heart, Rocky. Not without penalties.'

'I'm sorry,' he said, 'I have to.' And he started running back to the house.

I knew exactly what was coming next, and it didn't take a brilliant imagination—which, as I've said, I don't have—to know that it wasn't going to be fun.

Bad Tooth

As I watched him go I put my head in my hands, feeling an urge, for the second time in two days, to bang it against something very hard. Luckily there are no walls in a field, so I waded into the corn, shoving the plants away from me, just for the scratches they gave me back as I trampled the stalks, yelling at them, yelling at myself, 'Stupid! Stupid! Stupid!' And, for the first time I remember in years, crying real tears.

Then I was in the middle of the field and Klaris was talking to me. I couldn't interpret her the way Flea did, but I stopped and listened. She wanted me to go to the Island. I didn't know what else to do so I started walking in that direction. I half wondered if she was going to tell me to throw myself into the river, and I didn't even care.

But by the time I reached the riverside I felt different;

calm, like all the pieces of me were locked back into place again.

I sat down on the dusty bank, next to my dad's old wooden rowing boat, the *Lady Claire*, and stared over at Goat Island.

Most people around here call it Ghost Island but it's not really haunted. That rumour was started by the farmer to keep people off his fields. He doesn't own the Island though. It belongs to the Cliffs and us—it came with our houses.

We hadn't crossed that river for years. No one did any more, apart from some of Dr Cliff's friends who went over to shoot pigeons.

That day the Island looked inviting for once. All the trees were alive with green, apart from the tallest, an old sycamore that had been struck by lightning a couple of summers before, and stuck out like a bad tooth, with just a trail of white-flowering bindweed curled around its fat trunk.

I remembered that storm really well. It was my birthday and we nearly lost the boat too. It was found half a mile downstream a few days later. My dad bought a chain and padlock after that so it couldn't happen again.

I gave the *Lady Claire* a gentle kick and it rolled like a fat overexcited dog. I was going to do it again, harder, but then I spotted a charred stick, with a few dried-out sycamore seeds still attached, floating directly towards me. I fished it out and a long ribbon of weed came with it, dripping dank water down my arm and inside my T-shirt. I held it in the air for a moment, feeling the sensation of the water on my body, then pulled my arm back, flung the stick across the river, and watched it float away.

And I wished that I could've got Klaris out of my life that easily.

A Weird Kid Now

Everyone looked up as I entered.

Flea was sitting at the Cliffs' kitchen table, stiff and pale, with a cup of milky tea in front of him.

His mum smiled in my direction, but didn't make eye contact. So, I thought, it had happened. I was a weird kid now. It's amazing how fast everything can change.

'Hello, Joseph,' her voice sounded odd, forced. 'I, er, I think we need to have a word. Maybe you could come up to the study for a moment?'

I looked down at Rocky, who was shielding his cup of hot chocolate as if I might infect it with my weirdness. He shrugged his shoulders. There was no need to say anything. He'd broken his promise, but maybe I would have done the same thing. We all knew the facts. That most of them are fine, but sometimes, like with the rest of us, a crazy one develops—a rogue.

You have to look out for the signs. The little things you might not notice at first; the stuff being moved, things disappearing or getting broken. Then the run of bad luck; people getting sick, losing their jobs, marriages falling apart. Then they start migrating into other people.

And they have to be stopped before a tragedy happens. That's what they say anyway. I wanted Klaris out of my head, of course I did. But I didn't want the shame of people knowing. I didn't want the Cosh. And, I suppose, I didn't want to be the reason Flea's only friend had to go. Even if she was a pain in the neck.

Following Mrs Cliff up the dark stairs I could hear her husband's gravelly doctor's voice booming through the heavy door. He was a very large man, and the sound was amplified by his bulk.

We went in.

'Well, call me if he gets any worse. Goodbye.' Dr Cliff put down the phone and indicated that I should sit on the chair on the other side of the desk. He wasn't actually my doctor, but it felt, for a moment, like he was going to listen to my chest or ask about my bowel movements. Instead, he took off his glasses, cleaned them on the hem of his shirt, which was stretched tight across his belly, replaced them, and stared at me for a moment, before finally taking a deep breath and speaking.

'Joseph, Rocky has just told me something, and I need to ask you if it's true.'

I nodded.

'He said that Klaris has been talking to you.'

I squirmed in my seat.

'Well, not really . . .'

'But she has been contacting you?' He peered at a leaflet on the desk and read from it.

'"Making his/her presence known to you, with or without any encouragement, dual-controlling your thought processes for the purpose of communication and/or to influence your behaviour. Talking/singing/laughing/shouting at you."'

He looked up. 'Well? Has she? Has she done any of that?'

I was silent.

'See this?' He picked up a stethoscope that lay curled on his desk. He put the arms around his neck but the rubber tubing and metal disk stopped at his Adam's apple.

'She's removed a good six inches and stuck it back together so carefully that I didn't notice until it was too late. I suppose she thought it was a joke. Well, I can tell you, Mrs Jackson didn't think it was funny when I had to use it to listen to her chest. I'm surprised she didn't report me for gross misconduct.'

Dr Cliff dropped it down onto the desk and flopped back in his creaking leather chair. 'And then I find out today that she's graffiti'd her name on the back of the shed. Did you know that? Gouged it with a knife by the looks of things.'

I remembered the twins disappearing from view in the garden while I was watching from the apple tree.

'I think that was Wills and Egg.'

He batted the idea away with his blotchy hand. 'No, the twins can't write. They're refusing to learn. The school doesn't know what to do with them. Anyway, the point is she must have used a knife. A knife! How long before she's using weapons against *us*? She's getting bolder and bolder. First all these little things, and then . . .' He shot a glance at his wife, who glared back at him. 'Well, there's no need for you to know about that. The point is that she's set up a second home with you. She's migrating and we need to act quickly.'

'No, you're wrong.' I hated the way he'd already made up his mind with so little evidence. Almost as if he wanted her to be guilty. 'Klaris is harmless. She's not going to hurt anyone. She's not like that.'

He smiled a very professional smile. He'd trapped me. I really was useless at this.

'So, tell me, Joseph, what is she like?'

I shrugged. 'I don't know. A bit boring. Annoying sometimes, quite often actually. But usually, just really . . .' I knew it would sound pathetic before I even said it. 'Kind.'

'Kind? Kind!' His voice grew louder. 'You call this act of deliberate vandalism kind?' He waved the stunted stethoscope at me. I glanced over at Mrs Cliff, who was looking alarmed.

'No, course not.' I said quietly. 'I don't understand why she would've done that. Are you sure it wasn't someone else?' He gave me a frosty look, and there was silence for a moment. Then I had an idea. 'I've got a feeling she'll probably give up on me soon. So what about if we agree to leave it for a while? See how things are in a few weeks. Doctors always say that.'

He exhaled loudly. 'Not in this case, I'm afraid. Joseph, it's obvious that she's brainwashed you, and you're unable to think clearly, so there's no point in us discussing it further. We need to get on and do something. I'm going to call the Council for professional help.'

He picked up the leaflet. 'I think it's best to think of them like warts. You can wait for them to go, and meanwhile you risk infecting the whole family. Or you can,' he made a slicing motion, using the leaflet, over his throat, 'cut them out and prevent further problems.'

'But what about Flea?' I asked. 'Klaris is his best friend.'

He leaned back in his seat again, and looked me straight in the eye.

'You're going to have to trust me, Joseph. He'll make new friends.' His voice was firm, 'With real people,' and he passed me the leaflet. 'Take this home and read it.'

Rogue Imaginary Person Service (RIPS)
UNWANTED IMAGINARY PERSON?
Diagnosis, Treatment and Aftercare

'And try not to worry. We'll have it sorted out in no time at all. It'll be like Klaris never happened.' He smiled that smile again, turned away and started tapping at his computer. I left the room and closed the door. But before I walked away I heard Mrs Cliff's voice.

'You can't go blaming Klaris for our problems, Joe.'

'Hmm, can't I? Well, you'll see. Once she's gone, we'll be back to normal.'

Basketball on the Moon

Back at home I barged through the door, my eyes blurred with tears.

'Steady on there, Joseph,' said my dad, looking up from the computer. He saw my face. 'What's wrong?'

'Nothing.'

He got up from the sofa and came over to me. 'What sort of nothing?'

I paused. He'd find out soon enough. Dr Cliff would tell him. Even if he didn't, RIPS would need my dad's permission for treatment. But until then I couldn't bear to spoil his happiness. He'd been cheerful recently, and I didn't want to see that look back on his face; the saggy kicked-dog expression he'd had for months when mum didn't come back. The same one he used to wear when she acted weird, when she wouldn't get up for days, or wouldn't stop crying. I needed someone around me to be happy

61

and strong and just normal. Even if I had to lie to get it.

'It's Klaris. Flea's dad definitely wants to get rid of her.'

'And you're upset for young Flea?'

I nodded, feeling guilty as hell.

He pulled me towards him and gave me a long, tight hug.

My voice was muffled in the warm fabric of his T-shirt as I asked, 'Dad, you know the Cosh?'

'Hmm.'

'How do they do it? How exactly do they kill them?'

I could feel Klaris in the pause before he replied, flooding me with her pain. And I wished she'd keep her feelings to herself.

'They . . . they, er, they reduce the environment they live in. It's a bit like with pandas—if you cut down too much bamboo they die out.'

'Bamboo? What are you talking about?'

He sighed and let go of me. 'I suppose you're old enough to know the details now. But don't go telling Flea and frightening him unnecessarily.' He rubbed his forehead so hard it left white traces. 'As I understand it they wire you up to a brain scanner to find out exactly which area lights up when you use your imagination, and they . . . well, they reduce it.'

'What, they cut it out with a knife?'

He shook his head. 'No, not a knife, they use a laser. They zap the area and make it . . . shrivel.'

'Shrivel?'

'Well, I'm not sure *shrivel*'s the medical term. The idea isn't to completely kill it, just shrink it so nothing can live there.'

I resisted the urge to put my hands over my head.

'So, how much are you left with? Enough to make stuff up? Enough so you can still daydream?'

He shook his head slowly.

I let this sink in for a moment, thinking about what it would mean.

I'd never be able to imagine myself wing-walking on a biplane.

Or playing basketball on the moon.

Or diving with sharks.

I'd never be able to come up with fantastic inventions to save the planet.

And then, as if a shadow had fallen on me, I realized something else.

I'd never be able to imagine my mum coming back.

I wouldn't be able to see her, and hear her and feel her and even smell her whenever I wanted. I'd still have my memories, but they had already faded so pale that they weren't really like her any more.

She'd be gone. Completely gone this time.

I jumped up and ran as fast as I could straight back round to the Cliffs' house.

Flea and Rocky were still sitting at the kitchen table.

The two brothers looked up at me. Rocky with an embarrassed smirk, and Flea with a sad smile. I stood blocking the doorway staring straight at Rocky. He was my best friend, but he knew the rules. Our rules.

'I suppose you remember the punishment for breaking a solemn promise?' I said.

'What?' He was eating toast, and I could see the mushed up buttery mess in his mouth as he chewed.

I turned a chair round and sat straddling it with the back against my chest.

'You crossed your heart and licked the spit, Rocky. So, you've gotta face the consequences—the number ten.'

He put his forehead on the table and groaned. 'I know. I know. I deserve it.'

While he was down there I took his last slice of toast from the plate.

'Can't say I blame you, really. But rules are rules. And you did break the biggy.'

He sat up again, picked a few crumbs off his T-shirt, and ate them. 'So, I suppose I'm your slave for the week. Could be worse. Unless you're gonna throw me to the lions or something?'

'Nah. Lucky for you we're out of lions. But I might need your help. Because thanks to your big mouth we've got a problem. Me and Flea are gonna get coshed.'

'Yeah, I know, but she's migrating, Joseph. She's dangerous.'

'That's where you're wrong, brainiac. Klaris isn't dangerous. She's just a pain. OK, I admit she's somehow got into my head, but she's seriously not the type to do anything bad. Even *you* call her a wimp. Anyway, you've given your dad the ammunition he needed to get rid of her.'

Rocky thought again. 'You sure she's not dangerous?'

'Not unless you include being dangerously boring and helpful. She wakes me up in the morning when it's time for school, she reminds me to do my homework, she even finds socks I've lost. Not exactly your typical killer rogue profile. Unless her plan is to fuss us all to death.'

'Hmm . . .' Rocky still had his considering face on. It was a bit less extreme than his confused face, but still not a good look.

'Whatever, we don't want to get coshed, and Flea doesn't want to lose Klaris, so, as you're my slave I command you to help us.'

Rocky rubbed his buttery hands through his stubbly hair. 'OK. So what are we gonna do?'

I tried to sound confident. 'We're going to prove that Klaris Cliff is innocent.'

Unnaturally Tidy

We waited until Dr Cliff had gone out for a newspaper, then Rocky hacked his computer (Flea told us his password was PASSWORD—he deserved it) and printed out the letter that had been emailed to the Council about an hour before.

It was the usual: Dear Sir . . . Very concerned . . . imaginary person . . . in the light of Shorefield . . . blah blah blah. But the bit that interested us was the list on the second page.

It had grown.

```
1. Habitually turns on car lights and
      flats the battery
2. Vandalized my stethoscope
3. Killed the rabbit
4. Gave the dogs my whisky (the good
      stuff)
```

5. Carved her name into the back of the shed
6. Migrated into the boy next door
7. Is provoking serious marital disagreement

Flea clenched his fists. 'It's not true! None of it. She's being . . .' he searched for the right word. 'She's being *framed* by someone who hates her.'

'Maybe,' I said. 'But let's not jump to conclusions. We have to approach this like a detective would. We'll interview everyone in the house and find out what they know. And when we've got enough evidence we'll show it to your dad and he'll have to cancel RIPS.'

I saw a flash of sunlight on black hair as the twins swished past the open door.

'We may as well start with those two,' I said. 'I've got a feeling they're not as innocent as they look.'

Flea shook his head. 'My little brothers aren't at all innocent. They got suspended from school last term, and when they go back they've got to go into different classes.'

'Why?'

'Smoking.'

I laughed. Then I saw in his face that he was being serious.

'I think the teacher was cross because they sold cigarettes to the other kids for their lunch money.'

Rocky nodded and carried on the story.

'Stupid idiots got caught when no one could pay for their school dinners. My mum went mad.'

'Well, they were her cigarettes,' added Flea. 'I told her that if she gave up that would solve the problem. I reminded her of what Klaris always says, that she isn't setting a very good example for the little ones.'

'And what did she say to that?'

'She said that giving up wasn't easy. Then she went outside for a smoke.'

Pooh appeared at the door and stared at me for a second. Then she held the phone out to Rocky as if it was radioactive. 'Those idiot boys from the village for you,' she said before stalking out.

'Carry on without me,' said Rocky and left the room.

Flea pointed to number seven on the list.

'I think Mum and Dad are going to get divorced. I've heard them arguing about it.'

'Oh.' The snatch of conversation I'd heard through the door suddenly made sense. 'Don't worry, Flea. I'm sure they'll sort it out. My mum and dad used to argue sometimes.'

'But your mum's gone, hasn't she?'

I paused. 'Yeah, OK, bad example.'

Flea clamped his hand over his mouth. 'Sorry, Joseph, I didn't mean that.'

We were silent for a moment. I hoped that Flea was wrong about his parents. But it would explain why his dad was so worried about Klaris. She was fitting the classic rogue pattern, just the way it happened at Shorefield; first the minor things, all the stuff he was complaining about; the car lights, the stethoscope, the whisky. Then the bigger stuff: his marriage falling apart. Then the migration: that was me. And then . . . Well, I could see his point. But there was no time for pondering; if we were going to prove him wrong I needed to get a move on.

'So, who are we going to start with?'

'Try Pooh. I think she's in her room.'

I got up to go and he called me back. 'Joseph, catch.'

He threw me a pocket-sized tape recorder.

I whistled. 'A giant iPod with a tape. Where did you get this from?'

Flea tapped the side of his nose. 'It's called a Dictaphone, but the less you know about it the better.' He held out his tiny white hand for me to shake. It reminded me of a little bird and I took it gently, but his grip was firm.

'Good luck.'

I turned to go again, then paused. 'Flea, before I start, is there anything I should know about Pooh?'

He considered. 'Yes, there is. Something very important in fact.' He beckoned, and I moved closer. He spoke in a loud whisper. 'Pooh knows Klaris quite well. They used to play together.'

'They used to play together?' I repeated like a parrot,

thinking I had misheard him. 'Are you sure? I thought she only spoke to you.'

'It was ages ago,' he said. 'I'm over it.'

I walked slowly up the groaning stairs to Pooh's room. I hadn't been in there since I was little—well, not while she was at home anyway. Rocky sometimes went into her room to look for sweets, or just to nose about, but I always waited in the doorway. If it sounds like I was scared of Pooh, well, I probably was. Girls can be seriously scary sometimes.

I knocked at the door and it flew open. But, when she saw that it was me, Pooh paused and started closing it again, leaving just a six-inch gap to peer through.

'Er, Flea asked me to talk to you,' I said. 'Can I come in?'

She raised an eyebrow. How do girls learn to do things like that? It's a fact that boys have no control over their individual eyebrows, or any other non-essential body parts come to that.

'Is it true?' she asked through the gap.

'You mean about me and Klaris?'

'Yeah.'

''Fraid so. But,' I added, 'I don't think I'm contagious.'

She looked down, biting her lip in thought for a moment.

'You'd better not be,' she said, as she opened the door and stepped back to let me in.

Pooh's room was painted a dark pink—not the girly

colour, but a sort of deep raspberry shade, more like the inside of your mouth. And it was really tidy. I mean really unnaturally tidy. The books on the shelves were in colour order, and on the walls there were actual paintings in frames. Through the open window a warm breeze blew wind chimes, making an eerie tinkling sound.

'You can sit here,' she said, patting a space next to her on the bed, but I perched on the edge, worried about ruffling the covers.

I showed her the tape recorder. 'D'you mind if I use this?'

She shrugged, which I guessed meant go ahead, so I put it on the bed between us and pressed Record.

JR: Thanks for agreeing to help with this.

PC: What's going on, Joseph?

JR: Your dad's called in the Council. It could mean the Cosh for Flea and me.

PC: (Groans) I suppose he thinks she's going rogue?

JR: Er, yeah.

PC: Typical. I don't know what's up with him at the moment. He needs to learn to relax.

JR: So, you think he's overreacting? That's interesting.

PC: Of course he's overreacting.

JR: Anyway, I've got this list he's made, and I'm helping Flea prove she didn't do any of the things on it, and, well . . . I need to interview everyone in the family.

71

PC: (Silence) OK, as I've got nothing better to do. Go ahead. Ask me anything you want.

JR: Right, well, how did you first meet her?

PC: Meet her?

JR: Yes. Because if we can show she's not migrating, she just likes spending time with other people sometimes . . .

PC: What are you talking about?

JR: Oh, it's just that Flea . . .

PC: Flea what?

JR: He told me that you used to play with Klaris sometimes.

PC: He said what? The little worm! I'll kill him!

Square Minus One

I found the Dictaphone lying in the flowerbed.

The little plastic window was cracked. You could still see the tape but crumbs of soil rattled around inside. I pressed the Play button. Nothing. I was back at square one, or maybe square minus one. No interview and no interviewee. Not even a tape recorder.

'Hey, Joseph, is it OK?'

Typical of Flea to have witnessed the whole thing. 'Not really. Your sister's got a temper on her, hasn't she? I'd stay out of her way if I were you.'

He took the Dictaphone and turned it over in his hands.

'Hormones, my mum says. Did you know they're making her boobs grow too?'

'All right, enough detail.' Pooh was my friend, I couldn't start thinking of her as someone with boobs.

'Just let her cool off for a while, Joseph. I could set up

another interview for you. What about talking to my mum? She's in at the moment. Just doing the washing or something—nothing important. Or you could try the twins, but they're watching TV and they don't like being disturbed.'

My stomach fizzed. I really didn't want to speak to Flea's mum. Even if all the embarrassing stuff with Klaris hadn't happened earlier, I would've felt awkward. I suppose I was out of practice with mums.

But the thought of interviewing the twins was more than awkward. It was terrifying. What was happening to me? I was becoming nervous of my neighbours, the family I'd known since before half of them were even born.

'I need to go home and have a bit of a think. I have to be careful how I do this, Flea, because your family have always been my best friends, and I don't want anything to change that.'

He stared at me for a second, then turned away. He didn't look back, but he spoke as he walked. 'OK, Joseph. Just don't think for too long. I don't know how much time we've got.'

At home I went in through the open back door, slammed it shut behind me and threw myself onto the sofa. Well, that was the plan. But what I thought was a blanket over some cushions was actually my dad, asleep.

'What the—? Joseph! What did you do that for? You nearly broke my leg!'

'Sorry. But I didn't expect you to be lying here in the middle of the day.'

'I was tired. Up a bit late last night, so I thought why not have a little rest, and I must've nodded off.' He pulled up his trouser leg and rubbed his shin. 'You really cracked me one there.' He looked up, 'Are you all right, son?'

'Yeah. Y'know me—tough as anything.'

'It's just that you look a bit wound up. Have you fallen out with someone?'

'Well, yeah, I suppose you could say that.'

He sat up, moving the blanket so there was a space for me. 'Who was it? Rocky?'

'No. Pooh.'

He did one of those long, low whistles. 'How did you manage that?'

I thought for a moment, not wanting to give too much away. 'I obviously said the wrong thing, without realizing.'

'It's incredibly easy to say the wrong thing to women, Joseph. Actually, I'm thinking of writing a book based on my experiences of saying the wrong thing to your mother. It'll contain everything you can safely say to a woman without her taking offence.'

'Really? What'll be in it?'

'Nothing. All blank pages. Y'see, there are no safe topics, Joseph. Danger lies in the most unexpected places.'

He spread the blanket over both of us and pulled me close.

'Remind me never to get a girlfriend, Dad.'

'Will do, son. So, what did you say to upset Pooh?'

'Nothing. I just repeated something about her that Flea had told me.'

My dad breathed in sharply and shook his head, the way the mechanic had done when we took the car to the garage.

'Not usually a good move. You're safest letting the girl tell you all about herself first. People don't want to be prejudged; they want a chance to explain themselves. But don't ask her anything directly. Subtly bring the conversation round to the thing you want her to talk about then act like you don't care. She'll be dying to tell you.'

'So, let me get this right; she'll only want to tell me something I don't want to hear?'

He nodded.

'Are you sure?'

'Defo. Give it a go. If I'm wrong we'll eat takeaways for a week.'

'Pizza?'

'Well, not every night. You need a balanced diet. We'll have Chinese and Indian too.'

'Deal.'

White, Three Sugars

I'll do anything for pizza. Even face an angry Pooh.

OK, I know how funny that sounds, but you can blame her parents for giving her such a stupid name. Actually, they gave her a different stupid name then decided to call her Pooh for short. Child cruelty in my opinion.

Anyway, I headed next door and walked straight into the kitchen. The sun was blazing through the large windows, making it hot like a greenhouse, and Pooh was slumped over the table with her head resting on her arms. Her long hair was snaking out beside her, and a strand was lying just on the edge of a puddle of hot chocolate. I reached out, and, before I had time to think about what I was doing, I had gently moved it out of the way.

She sat up. 'Hey! What are you doing?'

'I just . . .' I pointed out the spilled drink. 'I didn't want you to get it in your hair.'

'Oh. Right, thanks.'

I went to leave but she stood up and walked over to the kettle. 'D'you want a cup of tea?'

'Yeah, OK. White, three sugars.'

'Three? You'll get fat.'

I ignored the comment, flicking through an old Batman comic on the table instead. I didn't even have to pretend to be engrossed because it was one I hadn't read before, so I'd sort of forgotten what I was meant to be doing by the time she handed me a mug and shoved the sugar bowl in my direction. Then there was an uncomfortable silence, just broken by Pooh coughing, as I tried to scrape up three spoonfuls, chipping away at the brownish crystals dried onto the bottom.

Finally Pooh said, 'So what are you going to do?'

I shrugged. 'The accusations are rubbish. I mean, someone's done it all, but definitely not Klaris. It shouldn't be too hard to prove she's innocent if people co-operate.'

She glared. 'I suppose you mean people like me?'

I sighed. 'It's up to you, Pooh. You can help if you want.'

'Of course I want to help. I don't want Flea to have the Cosh.' She paused, looking a bit embarrassed. 'Or you either. Just tell me what I have to do.'

She was practically begging. My dad was a genius. But, of course, she had one condition.

'You can't tell anyone I played with Klaris.'

I pretended to consider it, then nodded and cleared my throat.

'OK. So, er, Pooh.'

She interrupted. 'Shouldn't you call me Prudence Cliff if this is official?'

'Maybe. Yeah, OK, er, Prudence, strictly off the record, tell me about you and Klaris.'

Pooh started to cough again. I was worried that by the time she'd finished she might have changed her mind about helping. But the coughing fit subsided and she carried on.

'I was in the garden one summer, a couple of years ago, and the others were in the tree house. I think you were with them. You'd all made up a stupid gang, and Flea and me weren't allowed in.'

'Why was that?'

She was scowling. 'Rocky said it was boys only and I'm a girl.'

'So why wasn't Flea allowed?'

'Because he'd bring Klaris, and she's a girl too,' she glared at me. 'Obviously.'

'So what did you do next?'

'Flea went off somewhere, and I hung around at the bottom chucking stones up for a while. Then I got bored and wandered round the garden. That's when I pretended to notice Klaris. I sort of made up a game that she'd been following me.'

'You made it up?'

'Yeah, I think so. Well, I thought so at the time. Oh, I don't know. It's so hard to remember properly now. Anyway after a while it didn't feel like pretending any more. The game just sort of played itself. D'you know what I mean?'

I nodded. 'So, what did you and Klaris do?'

Pooh paused as she plucked a long pale hair from her T-shirt. 'Well after that first time we often used to just hang out together. And sometimes we'd go digging in the flowerbeds for bits of old pottery, worms, pretty stones, you know the kind of thing. I'd find something and show it to her. Sometimes we put them in little boxes I decorated and we buried them in the garden under the lavender.'

'What, the worms too?'

'No, we just let them slither away. And I remember we talked sometimes, but she was difficult to understand, a bit like someone talking through water. Actually . . .' she looked up suddenly. 'I've just remembered something strange.'

'What?'

'She talked about you.'

I gulped—I actually gulped like a cartoon character. 'Me? Are you sure?'

'Yeah. But I didn't really understand what she said. Sorry, I don't remember much more, apart from that I had fun, and it really annoyed Flea. I heard him shouting at Klaris once. He told her that she was his, and she shouldn't go off with other people.'

'And what did she say to that?'

'How do I know? I suppose she said OK because she hasn't gone off with other people, has she . . .' Pooh trailed, looking awkward. 'Well, not till now anyway.'

'Yeah . . .'

'I wonder why she didn't talk to you back then?'

I shrugged. 'You seen my English and art grades? I'm not the type. I'm not imaginative like you and Flea. I'm more the practical sort. I expect I was a tough nut to crack,' I tapped my skull. 'See, an impenetrable fortress. Well, almost.'

Pooh was looking thoughtful. 'But it's supposed to be harder for them to get in around our age. So if she couldn't get through to you two years ago, why would she bother with you now?'

I shook my head, taking the list out of my pocket. 'I wish I knew. Here, this is the stuff she's supposed to have done.'

Pooh had a quick look—perhaps too quick—and handed it back. 'Nope, nothing to do with me. Ask the twins. Looks more like their kind of thing.'

'Yeah, just what I thought.'

She chewed her lip, then spoke more softly. 'Flea must feel awful.'

'He does. He really loves her.'

She studied a strand of her hair, splaying the ends

like bristles on a paintbrush. 'I sort of understand why. She . . .' Pooh looked around, making sure no one else was listening. 'Don't tell anyone, but she was nice. When she played with me I felt sort of warm inside. Is it like that for you?'

I smirked. 'Not exactly.' Then I felt guilty and added, 'Well, she's not too bad I suppose. If you like that kind of thing.'

'I know what you mean. I still don't like Klaris hanging around here, it's totally embarrassing. But I hate that my dad would do this to her.'

I heard a door slam above us, then the dogs came down the stairs and into the room. The two big black Labradors' bodies wiggled from side to side like bendy buses, and their thick tails banged against my legs as they sniffed around the floor for food dropped at breakfast. Then one of them turned and began nuzzling at my legs, probably hoping I was hiding a bacon sandwich in my jeans pocket. To my horror he worked his nose up and started sniffing at my crotch.

'Oi, get off, you!'

Pooh laughed. 'Get down, Henry,' she said and tried to drag him off by his collar. But he kept coming back for more.

'I don't think I'll ever have a dog,' I said. 'I can't put up with all the bottom sniffing and drooling.' I looked at Annie, who, with her usual string of saliva stretching from her lip down past her chin, looked like she had a mild case of rabies. To make it even worse her belly now hung down where a litter of Henry's puppies was growing.

'Maybe I could have a small dog.'

'Like a chihuahua with a diamond collar?' Pooh sniggered.

'No, nothing girlie. A tough little terrier. At least if I had a small dog I wouldn't have to pick up great big dog's—'

I was going to say poohs, but I'd remembered just in time who I was talking to, and I didn't want to use her name like that.

'Doggy chocs? That's what my granny calls them.'

'Yuk. Yeah, at least little dogs would have tiny doggy chocs.' I patted Henry's head, then wiped my hands on my trouser legs. 'Actually, I was thinking I ought to interview the dogs too. I mean, they are involved. Number three on the list.'

Pooh laughed. 'So how are you going to do that?'

'Dunno.' I turned to face Annie. 'So, Annie Cliff, was it your idea to eat the poor innocent rabbit known as Barry White Cliff?' She sat alert, looking me in the eyes, and held up a paw.

'What does that mean?'

'It means she thinks you've got something for her.'

'Oh, demanding a bribe, are you? Won't squeal unless I grease your paw?'

I scooped a few abandoned Cheerios off the table and tossed her one, which she caught mid-air.

'Are you ready to talk now?' Annie barked in response. 'OK, then, did you tell Dr Cliff that Klaris made you do it?' Silence, just a paw raised and replaced impatiently, like a little stamp.

'Is that one for yes and two for no?' She repeated the action. 'Right, let's keep it simple; you gonna come clean an' take da rap?' The paw raised and fell twice. 'Hmm, well unless you do you could be looking at a stretch in the kennel.'

'Joseph, we haven't got a kennel,' whispered Pooh.

I shot her a glare. 'Shhh. Can't you see I'm putting the frighteners on them?'

I swept the remaining Cheerios into my hand and threw them on the floor where the dogs vacuumed them up in seconds.

'And there are plenty more where those came from if you remember anything useful.'

Pooh was smiling at me. 'You're enjoying this detective business, aren't you?'

'Not really. Henry and Annie are probably the most co-operative witnesses I've had so far. Anyway, what's the story with the rabbit?'

She scraped her chair back and stood up. 'Flea was devastated when Barry White was killed. He was the only one of us that really took any notice of him once the novelty wore off. He used to set up challenges for him with tunnels and bits of carrot, stuff like that.'

'Do rabbits like challenges?'

'Doesn't everyone?' She picked up my empty cup and took it to the sink. 'Anyway,' she ran the tap and started on the washing up, 'it was one evening. Flea went to the loo and left Barry alone in the living room and somehow the French windows got opened.'

'Who did that?'

'We don't know. I think it was probably the twins, but my Dad's certain that somehow it was Klaris. He thinks she let the dogs in and forced them to kill the rabbit. He won't admit that they might have had the idea themselves. But you know he loves those dogs more than he loves his own wife and kids.'

I must've looked shocked.

'It's true. I don't think Mum and Dad have spoken to each other without shouting for about a year. And Dad just ignores us. You've heard me coughing, haven't you?' I nodded. 'Well, he refuses to listen to my chest. He just says "there's a lot of it about. You'll survive." But if it was those dogs he'd whip his stethoscope out straight away.'

I needed to get her back onto the topic of Klaris. 'So did the dogs actually eat the rabbit?'

'Well, we presume so. All that was left was a little blood stain on the rug.'

'Poor Barry, and poor Flea too. Y'know, I think he's really lonely.'

Pooh snorted, her mood changing suddenly. 'Lonely? Try being the only girl in a house with four brothers, and a dad who hardly notices you exist.'

She must've detected a slight movement in my face, something I didn't want her to see, because she put her arm around me.

'Sorry Joseph, that wasn't very sensitive. It must be awful for you since . . .'

'It's OK.' I stood, enjoying the weight of her arm over my shoulders for a moment until we both realized with a jolt what we were doing and sprung apart.

'Anyway, I'd better go,' I said. 'Thanks for talking to me.'

'If you need my help again, just ask.'

I walked to the door.

'I mean it, Joseph. I know Flea's lonely and I am sometimes really horrible to him, but I'm his big sister. That's what sisters do, isn't it?'

I shook my head. 'I wouldn't know, Pooh.'

I turned to go, but she called me back.

'Wait a sec. I've got something for you.'

I flushed. I don't know why, but, just for a second— no, way less than a second—I thought she was going to give me a kiss. At least I didn't shut my eyes and pucker up. But only just.

She ran upstairs to her room and came back with something in her hand. She held it out to me. It was a little pot of superglue.

I must've looked confused.

'For your investigation—evidence I think it's called.'

I remembered her dad waving his stethoscope around and saying, 'She's stuck it back together so carefully that I didn't notice until it was too late.'

'Thanks,' I said and I ran back home before I made an idiot of myself.

A Big Boozy Kiss

Back at home Dad was still hunched over the computer. I wondered if he was becoming an Internet addict, one of those people who spend all their time online while their families starve to death. At least I had the Cliffs, who would feed me if things got really bad. Well, I hoped they would anyway.

I heard a tap at the window and saw a thin pale face peering through the mottled pane. The apparition grinned and tapped again, doing the 'tap tap tap-tap tap—tap tap' thing. I went to the open door and stuck my head out.

'Come in, Flea.'

'Right,' he said, his smile gone. 'I think you should interview Rocky next.'

'Er . . .' Flea knew as well as I did that Rocky wouldn't like being treated like a suspect.

'We have to interview everyone, Joseph. Except each other of course.'

'I know. But he's already seen the list. Is there anything else I need to ask?'

'We need to know . . .' He pushed his downy hair out of his eyes and tucked it behind his ears. 'We need to know why he hates Klaris.'

Rocky took the news as well as I had expected.

'Oh, mate, this had better be a joke!' He was shaking his head in a kind of you-killed-my-kitten way. 'I've got nothing to do with it, and you know it.' A fragment of wet crisp flew at me from his mouth and landed on my cheek. Cheese 'n' onion, of course. 'I thought I was helping you sort this out. I thought I was on Team Klaris.'

I wiped the crisp off. 'Actually, Rocky, in case you've forgotten, you're my slave for the week, and I haven't even asked you to lick my shoes clean yet, so I don't think you should complain.'

He turned back to *Thief School*, the reality TV show about burglars that he'd been watching, and laughed as a trainee criminal fell off a drainpipe.

'Look, Rocky, I've got to interview everyone so we can do a proper investigation. If we get it wrong, me and Flea are for the you-know-what.'

He ignored me, so I put the tips of my fingers to my scalp and made a loud buzzing sound.

He grimaced. 'Don't do that. It's sick.'

I buzzed again.

'No, don't do it!'

Of course I did it again.

'OK, OK, I'll do your stupid interview.'

'You mean I'll do your stupid interview, Master.'

'Yeah, whatever.'

I dropped my hands from my head.

'Not that I've done anything wrong,' he added.

'No one's saying you have, Rocky. Anyway, I'm just trying to get some background on her, so why don't you tell me what you know about Klaris.'

He shrugged. 'She's an annoying little nerd who tells tales and spoils everyone's fun.'

'In what way?'

'Oh, I don't know. But everything's better when she's not around.' He paused. 'That doesn't mean I want her coshed though.'

'Never said you did.'

'Good. Because I wouldn't want to harm anyone. Not even annoying little nerds. Well, not unless I was in the army, then I would because that would be my job and I'd shoot them between the eyes.' He made his hand into a pistol and peered through an imaginary sight. 'BAM! BAM! BAM!' The pistol became a hand again. 'But only if they were the enemy, obviously.'

I couldn't let Rocky get sidetracked by his favourite subject. 'Can we talk about Klaris a bit more?'

'What? Oh, yeah.' He picked something green from his large white front teeth and wiped it on his trousers. 'Well, I suppose I don't really like way she controls Flea. It's not normal.'

'What do you mean, not normal?'

'She . . .' He paused.

'She what? Does she make him do things?'

He laughed. 'No.'

'What then?'

'She makes him *not* do things. Normal things.'

'What d'you mean?'

'It's like this: Flea's my brother. I know he's four years younger than me, but he's still my closest brother. And he never wants to hang out with me, or do stuff I enjoy cos Klaris tells him not to.'

'What sort of stuff?'

'You know, knocking on doors and running away. Or playing tricks on Pooh. Or even swimming. Did you know Klaris won't let Flea go swimming?'

I shook my head. 'I just thought he didn't like it.'

Rocky leaned forward. 'No, Flea used to love swimming. A proper little water baby. Then he stopped. Now he just paddles around the shallow end of the pool like a toddler, and everyone stares at him. It's really embarrassing.'

'And you don't know what put him off?'

Rocky scratched his head, then examined his nails. 'I suppose it was when . . .' He dropped his voice. 'I did something, and I got into massive trouble at the time, which was totally out of order. You must remember.'

'No, you're going to have to remind me.'

He mumbled. 'I held him under the water and he nearly drowned.'

'Oh, that. Yeah, I remember. So why did you do it?'

'It was no biggie really. I'd brought my surfboard down to the pool, but they wouldn't let me take it in. I was pretty annoyed, so . . . So I thought I'd use my initiative and make myself one instead.'

'Out of your brother?'

'Exactly. He wasn't busy, so I thought, why not? Anyway, he went a funny colour, then he coughed a lot and threw up all over the side of the pool. It was really rank.'

'And where was Klaris?'

'I don't think she was there that day.'

'But she's been there every time since?'

'Yeah.'

This wasn't helping, so I took out the piece of paper.

'Rocky, don't take it the wrong way, but did you do any of the stuff on this list?'

He took my pen and studied the list. He ticked something, and turned back to watch a contestant hot-wiring a car. 'So that's how you do it,' he said. 'I've always wondered.'

I looked at the list. He had ticked number four.

'Rocky, why did you get the dogs drunk?'

He was still looking at the TV but I thought I saw him twitch. 'It was in a good cause. My dad would probably thank me if he knew the reason.'

'Yeah, and?'

He unglued his eyes from the programme, but, instead of looking my way, he fixed his gaze on a tiny hole in his trousers and started picking at it. 'Y'know my dad's always fancied himself as a Labrador breeder? My granddad bred this whole load of Crufts champions and Dad's still got the trophies in his study. That's why he bought Annie—she's from some pedigree-winning line. Trouble is Henry's not interested in her like that. He just wants to be friends.' Rocky raised his head and I was surprised to see him looking upset. 'Every time Annie has a season my dad gets really annoyed when she doesn't get preggers.'

I nodded, but still had no idea where this was going.

'Well, it was just before we broke up for the holidays, and Annie was ready and Henry was ignoring her again, and Dad was in a really foul mood about it, worse than he'd ever been before, and taking it out on us lot cos his dog wasn't feeling frisky. So then I had a brainwave. Y'know how they say alcohol can make you do things you'll regret? Well, I thought I'd try it with the dogs. Y'know, to get them in the mood for love.' He grinned at the memory. 'It worked too. Annie's about to drop a litter, and Dad's slightly less grumpy. Well, he was until all this Klaris business happened.'

'So win, win,' I said. 'Except that somehow your dad found out.'

'Yeah, well that's Henry's stupid fault. Dad would never have known anything about it if Henry hadn't also felt extra loving towards him and given him a big boozy kiss.'

I wasn't looking forward to explaining this to Dr Cliff.

'I've got to ask you, Rocky; apart from the whisky, did you do anything else on this list?'

He took it from me again, went through it slowly, his mouth moving as he read, and handed it back.

'Nope. I swear on my alcoholic dogs' lives that I didn't.'

I shoved a piece of paper forward. 'Write and sign your confession here.'

He wrote 'I did the whisky one. Sorry.' And signed his name with a smiley face in the O and a flourish on the end of the Y.

Then he said, 'If you don't mind, I think I'll leave the rest of the investigating to you. I mean, I'll help if you need me, but it's not really my kind of thing.'

I took the confession from him and tried to look disappointed.

'It's all right, Rocky. I know you're busy. We'll try to manage.'

Flea peered around the living-room door.

'Are you two finished?'

'Get out,' said Rocky. 'Leave the real people alone.'

I suppose I expected Flea to run out, or at least look upset. But he didn't. He just stared at Rocky as if he was an exhibit in a zoo.

Rocky stared back for a moment, then his eyes darted away and he mumbled, 'Flea. I . . . Er . . . I'm sorry for nearly drowning you that day.'

Flea stared again for a second, then gave a tiny nod and walked out.

I found him sitting on the back doorstep and I squeezed myself in between his bony hip and the doorframe.

'Good news, Flea—I've got a signed confession for the whisky.'

'Great.' He didn't sound very happy.

'What's up?'

'Nothing really. It's just . . . It's just that I'd forgotten about the drowning thing, and now I'll have to remember it all over again.'

I sighed. 'It was a long time ago, Flea. And he wasn't actually *trying* to kill you, you know? He was just being Rocky.'

Flea shut his eyes, made a steeple with his fingers, and breathed in and out deeply through his nose.

'That's what Klaris says too. She says he can't help it, he's just immature. She says that swimming is good exercise and I should put it behind me and go and enjoy myself.'

I put my arm over his spiky shoulders.

'He did say sorry, you know. I think he really meant it.'

Flea tried a wobbly smile. 'Yes, he did, didn't he?' He thought for a moment. 'Maybe I'll start to forgive him soon.'

'Good. Anyway, I'm going to go home for a bit. Will you be OK here by yourself?'

He looked confused. 'But I'm not by myself, Joseph. Klaris is here, silly.'

And then I saw the ants on the step, bouncing away as if there was a bug-proof force field around our feet.

And I felt her talking to me, and I think she said something like, 'Just get on with it, Joseph.'

Like Creamed Spinach

Back at home I sat on the sofa and wrote out Pooh and Rocky's interviews in an old exercise book. Then I stuck Rocky's confession in with the glue Pooh had given me.

My dad came in carrying my school shoes.

'Look at these. The stitching's gone, Joseph. I think we're going to have to get you some new ones. We don't want you going back to school looking like an extra from Oliver.'

'Yeah. They're a bit small anyway. I reckon I'm a seven or eight now.'

My dad loosened the frayed laces and pulled out the tongue. He screwed his eyes up to read the label.

'These are a six. How come your feet have grown so fast?'

'They're just keeping up with the rest of me. I'm about four inches taller than when we got those shoes. If my feet hadn't grown too I'd probably fall over.'

'Good point, Joseph, good point. Well, we're going to town anyway, so we'll get you measured. We don't want your toes growing crooked. Your mum would never forgive me.'

I felt like saying she's not here, so she can't really have any opinion on the shape of my toes, can she? They could curl right up like court jester's shoes, with a bell on the top, for all she cares. But I just thought it instead, because no matter how good it might feel to say stuff like that, I know that none of it's his fault. It never was.

'Anyway, the shoe shop's right next to those trendy men's clothes shops. I'm hoping we might find something good for me to wear on Friday night.'

'You must be serious about this woman to actually be buying new clothes.'

'Cheeky little sod! I buy new clothes all the time. It's just that I'm not a fashion victim, that's all. I prefer to stick to the classics: you can't go wrong with black jeans, a well-fitting T-shirt, perhaps featuring an iconic rock band, and a pair of worn-in Doc Martins. Because real style, my son, never goes out of fashion.'

'Yeah, Dad. Whatever you say.'

I helped him find his wallet and keys and then we headed out to the driveway. I hoped that he was going towards his relatively new white work van. But no, it had to be the car. Traveling in style he calls it. Seriously. It had probably always been an embarrassing vehicle; a thirty-year-old canary-yellow Ford Capri with black 'go-faster' stripes along the side and bucket seats. But now it was far beyond embarrassing and well into the total-humiliation zone. One consolation was that the seats were low and the windscreen tinted, so no one could actually see me.

I got in and shut the door carefully so that nothing dropped off. If it was bad from the outside, that was nothing compared with the interior. The car hadn't dried out properly from the winter before, and it smelled like compost. I scraped my fingernail along the green-encrusted window seal and examined its contents. It looked like creamed spinach, which was another thing I hadn't seen since Mum had gone.

Dad got in and started the throaty engine.

I held up my finger to show him. 'Did you know there's moss growing inside the windows?'

'Yep. Most people have a sound system in their car, Joseph. We have an ecosystem.'

'Very funny. But it is rank in here.'

He sighed. 'Yeah, I know.'

As we crunched slowly out of the drive, Dad going at his usual two miles an hour so he didn't hit any stray Cliff kids, Flea appeared. He came running over to the car and I carefully wound down the window.

'Where are you going, Joseph?' His face was more

deathly pale than usual, and he was bobbing on his tiptoes.

'Town.' I shook my head and my fringe flopped into my eyes. 'I need a haircut.'

He held up a newspaper. 'Look here, on the front page.' I parted my fringe. 'Klaris spotted it. She likes to keep up with what's going on.'

TRAGIC DEATH OF LOCAL MAN –
IMAGINARY PERSON SUSPECTED

My good mood disappeared back to wherever it usually lived.

'Can I take it?'

Flea passed the newspaper through the window and stepped back as we pulled out of the driveway. In the wing mirror I could see him standing on tiptoes waving.

I read silently as Dad drove.

Peter White, 38, has been found dead at his family home on West Vale Drive. A police spokesperson has stated that they are yet to discover the cause of death, but neighbours have spoken exclusively to this newspaper reporting concerns over an imaginary person living with White's six-year-old daughter, Verity.

One local resident, who did not wish to be named,

told us, 'It was that Mr Sparks, we all know it. He was always up to something. He was evil. Little Verity, bless her, she couldn't control him. We warned Pete, but he wouldn't listen. Said he was harmless. And now look what's happened.'

White is known to have suffered from a heart condition, though he is thought to have been well recently.
It is understood that the family have agreed to Verity undergoing the imaginary person removal procedure known as the COSH, as a precautionary measure.

My dad must've seen the headline—it was big enough—but he stayed silent as I read. When I'd finished, and folded the paper shut on Mr White's smiling face, Dad said, 'Anything you want to talk about?'

I shook my head.

'So they're blaming a rogue?'

'Yeah.'

He slowed down at the roundabout. 'I expect you're thinking this is going to make things harder for Flea, aren't you?'

I didn't answer.

'It's just the local rag, Joseph. I wouldn't worry about it. I'm sure it'll turn out the poor chap already had some sort of health problem.'

'How did you know that?'

'Just a guess. It's what newspapers do. They get everyone stirred up about nothing. Anyway, you don't need to lose any sleep over it on Flea's behalf. Dr Cliff's a medical man, a scientist. Stories like this won't affect his decision one way or the other.'

I wanted to believe that he was right. But all the same I had to grip my knees to stop them from shaking.

It was dusk as we drove back from town, and I felt full and sick.

We'd ended up at Don Giovanni's Pizza Emporium, and, instead of Dad trying to fob me off with the Bambino Meal—a six-inch pizza, and measly bowl of ice cream with slimy red sauce—he'd handed me the menu and said I could have whatever I wanted. Obviously he was on safe ground, he knows I only like margheritas, but I still appreciated it.

It almost made up for the fact that while I just had new school shoes, and a bad haircut, my dad had expensive aftershave and a fancy carrier bag with rope handles, crammed with origami-folded new clothes for his date.

I couldn't stop him buying his usual black jeans, but then I found a cool purple shirt with a white pattern. It wasn't his usual kind of thing, and he was just holding it against himself and frowning into a mirror when a shop assistant tried to take it away to give to a young bloke standing near the changing rooms. Of course then my dad decided he did want it, and he marched straight up to the till waving his credit card.

He was still gloating when we were driving home.

'Did you see his face when I bought it, Joseph? Did you see it?'

'Yeah. I saw it, Dad.'

'I'm going to look great in this lot on Friday. Ten years younger. I reckon this could be the start of a new phase for me. I can feel it in my waters.'

Deer!

'Deer!'

My dad slammed the breaks on and the car skidded so violently to the right that only the seatbelt stopped me flying onto his lap. Half a second later a huge tan-coloured deer ambled onto the road and stopped right in front of us staring, its eyes white discs reflecting our headlights.

'Bloody hell, that was a close one,' Dad said as the deer turned and trotted away into the woods on the other side of the road. 'Thanks for the warning, son. We wouldn't have liked him coming through the windscreen, would we, eh?' He patted the dashboard and I realized he was talking to his car. Then he turned to me, tilting his head to one side. 'I don't know how you saw it though, Joseph. You must have much better eyesight than me. Shows how much I need those new glasses.'

'Er, yeah,' I replied. 'It's probably because it's dusk. Hard for old eyes to adjust to this sort of light.'

But I hadn't seen the deer any earlier than him. It was just lucky for us that Klaris had. She'd saved us from a nasty accident. And, although it did occur to me that she had also saved the stinking old Capri, I was grateful.

'Thanks, er, Klaris,' I mouthed into the rank air of the car.

And from somewhere near the back of my mind I felt her say, 'You're welcome.'

But there was more I needed to say, so I wound down the window and whispered into the breeze.

'I'm going to save you, I promise. Not just for us. For you too. You're not . . . You're not that bad really.'

But, when we got home and stepped inside the house, my certainty trickled away like water down a drain.

There was a note addressed to me on the mat. I turned it over. It said:

RIPS coming Friday at 4 o'clock. We only have 2 full days left. Time is running out. Meet 9 am tomorrow.

Flea
X

WEDNESDAY

Digger's Wheeze

By the time I'd staggered downstairs the next morning, still in my shortie pyjamas and dressing gown combo, Dad and Flea were in the middle of a card game.

'Hey, sleeping beauty. Flea here tells me you had a meeting arranged for this morning. He says you're helping him with his, er, problem.'

'Yeah, sort of.' I could tell from my dad's face that Flea hadn't told him the full story. 'What are you playing?'

Flea looked up from his cards, his face expressionless. 'Poker.'

'You serious?'

'Never more,' said Dad. 'And young Flea here seems to know what he's doing, so please take him away before he cleans me out completely.'

Flea laid down his cards and swept up a tower of coins. It was mostly two and five pence pieces, but it made an impressive pile on the table.

'Thanks, Flea,' said Dad. 'We'll do that again soon. When I've saved up a bit.'

'Any time.' Flea turned to me. 'Here, you can have this. It's your wages.'

I pushed it away. 'No. I don't want your money Flea.'

'Go on, Joseph,' said Dad. 'It'll make him feel better if he's paying you for your help.'

Flea was nodding, but I didn't want to take it. Surely he knew I was only helping him because I didn't want to get my head zapped too? I decided on a compromise.

'OK, Flea, how about we take it to the shop and spend it together?'

Smith's Village Convenience Store is about twenty minutes from home; close enough to walk to, but far enough to stop us going too often.

There's no pavement on the road into the village, so we trudged in single file along the narrow grass verge. We didn't talk because the ground's so uneven that if you don't concentrate you can twist your ankle. Plus, every time a car comes past the whoosh of air carries your sentence away with it.

So I stumbled along thinking about how to tackle the twins. One thing was certain, I wasn't going to fall for the sweet-little-boys act. I just had to get the approach right. But how do you get the truth out of two five-year-olds who barely speak to anyone apart from each other?

I was still wondering how I should play it when we arrived at the shop. I pushed open the door and the 'bing-bong' of the new electronic bell was almost drowned out by canned laughter coming from somewhere behind the counter. A minute or so later we were staring at the range of dusty chocolate bars and scary dried fruits, when the red beaded curtain that led to the back jangled and Terri Bickle stepped through like Moses parting the Red Sea.

Terri was in the year above me, and famous at school, but not in a good way. She squeezed behind the counter, and leaned towards us, her blackcurrant eyes running over our bodies, checking to see if we'd shoved anything into our pockets while she was in the back. Then a confused look passed over her face, and her mouth opened and hung for a second, revealing her spit-encrusted braces.

'Joseph Reece, that ain't your brother, is it?' she said to me. 'The little kid what talks to 'maginary people?'

I shook my head and continued to look for something worth spending Flea's winnings on.

'Fought not.' She beckoned for me to come closer, but I stayed where I was, so she said it anyway. 'You wanna be careful hanging around wiv 'im and that fing.'

I grabbed some overpriced crisps, vegetarian jelly snakes and chocolate buttons, slammed the money onto the counter, stuffed the food into my pockets, and we marched out without our change.

But once we'd left the shop I didn't know where to go.

'Why not the park?' Flea suggested.

It was the obvious place, but I shook my head. 'It'll be too crowded.'

Flea thought about my answer for a while, then said, 'I know it's embarrassing to be seen with me. I'm sorry.'

'I'm not embarrassed.' I spoke too fast. It was obviously a lie. I booted a Pepsi can out of my way, avoiding Flea's gaze.

'OK,' he said, 'but, if you were, I wouldn't mind, that's all. I'm used to it.'

'It's not you, Flea. It's just that some of the kids who hang around the park are total losers.'

'OK, why don't we go to the graveyard? There's never anyone there, unless . . .' Flea whispered. 'Unless there's a funeral on.'

'The graveyard? Why not.'

The rusty gates of the St Aloysius Cemetery creaked as we pushed them open, and left sharp little flecks of paint sticking in our hands. But once we were inside, and bats didn't darken the sky, I began to relax a bit. It was turning into another hot day and I didn't think the undead would risk being fried by the sun just to freak me out.

I was becoming so relaxed that I even suggested we climb up and sit on one of the crumbling old tombs, but

Flea said it was disrespectful, so we chose a bench near some of the newer gravestones. I passed Flea the chocolate buttons, and opened my crisps, but I kept the jelly snakes in my pocket. I was planning to use them later.

We sat in silence. Flea liked sucking the chocolate buttons slowly and wouldn't move or talk until they'd melted. Not that I wanted to chat anyway. I stretched out my legs and enjoyed the duet of the birds singing and my crisps crunching, and I wondered if either of us would end up buried here. I looked at some of the names on the gravestones; the Humphreys, Turners, and Johnsons. No Reeces. Reece is a Welsh surname, and we were a long way from Wales.

As I sat there listening to the bass notes of the pigeons and the high chirrups and squawks of the sparrows squabbling, I tuned into something else—Klaris was chatting. But not to me or Flea. It was like listening to one side of a phone conversation. I was definitely getting better at understanding her words, but, for the second time, I could also feel snatches of her emotions; sadness, joy, amusement. I realized that she was in my head, but sometimes, just a little bit, I was in hers too.

Flea was listening as well, but he didn't look surprised. 'She knows some of them,' he said, staring over the cityscape of white tombstones. 'She doesn't like to talk about her past, but I think she used to live in the village.'

Of course I knew that Klaris must've been alive once. She was no different to any other imaginary person. They live, they die, they float around for a bit, days, years, centuries, then, for some reason, they nip into an unsuspecting kid's brain while they're busy imagining fairies or playing superheroes.

But knowing something as a fact that you would learn at school, like where eggs come from, and actually admitting that fact to yourself when you're tucking into your breakfast, are two different things. So I had never let myself think of this person buzzing around in my nice new twenty-first century head as some mouldy old Victorian or Tudor.

But that day, in the bright sunshine, everything seemed better, more bearable, so I started scanning the tombstones to see if I could spot her name.

'Flea, how d'you spell Klaris?'

He shrugged. 'I was little when she came, and she told me I could spell it however I wanted, so I spell it K-L-A-R-I-S. Why?'

'Oh, nothing.'

It was then that I heard Digger's wheeze. Through the trees I spotted his body, low and gleaming, like a well-polished mahogany coffee table, hurtling towards us and dragging Tyler Jones and his little brother Ethan behind. The dog raised his nose from the ground as he saw us, and when the boys dropped the lead he ran up and smeared me with foaming drool.

Tyler shouted over. 'Joseph! Flea! You come wid us.' He'd obviously been practising his gangsta speak. 'Dey said to bring you to da park.' He pointed at Flea. 'Dey got sumting to show you.'

He shoved his brother Ethan, a smaller version of himself, from the blond crew cut with zig-zag patterns shaved into the sides, down to his pointed, freckled nose. 'Init, Eef!'

Ethan nodded. 'Yeah, just like Ty said.'

Flea turned to me, but I shrugged—I didn't know what was going on either. We didn't move, so Tyler grabbed Flea by the arm and started pulling him out of the churchyard. I'm bigger and older, so I should've just pushed Tyler off, but suddenly Digger's sharp-toothed smile looked threatening. So I decided that a friendly approach might be better.

'Let go of him, Tyler, and we'll come with you.' I said. 'We haven't got anything better to do anyway.'

He dropped Flea's arm. 'Jes don't you tink of runnin', or else.'

K for Killer

We all walked together, with Digger circling us, down the road that led to the park.

As we came through the stone gateway Tyler pointed to the wooded area behind the swings. 'Dis whey,' he said. And there we saw five teenage boys standing in a row facing us, arms folded and scowling. The oldest, Charlie Frazer, six foot tall already, with greasy black hair and a dirty shadow where his first moustache was waiting, stepped forward.

'I'm glad you two are here,' he said. 'I've got a little problem.'

The human wall parted to reveal a bike. Just an ordinary racing bike.

Flea looked confused. 'What's wrong with it?' He took a step closer. 'Has the chain come off? Because Rocky knows how to fix that. He does it with dessert spoons. I could ask him if you like.'

Charlie went over to the bike, picked it up, and, holding the back wheel off the ground, turned the pedal. The wheel purred as it spun.

'Nope, not the chain. See, working perfectly.' He put his hand on the tyre, stopped the wheel, and stared at Flea. 'Just like it was when I went flying down that hill yesterday.'

'So what's the problem?' Flea asked, not seeming to notice the atmosphere, which was unnaturally still.

'Oh, just this little thing,' said Charlie, pulling the back brake lever. It clunked, then, as he let go, it hung open uselessly, frayed cable poking out from both ends.

'Oh, yes,' said Flea. 'That could be very dangerous.'

Charlie's face twisted. 'Just what I thought as I went headfirst over the handlebars and nearly smashed my brains all over the road. Very dangerous.'

'You're lucky you weren't badly hurt,' said Flea.

I suddenly realized where this was leading.

'It's got nothing to do with him, Charlie,' I said. 'Come on, Flea, let's go.'

The boys stepped forward. 'You're not going anywhere till I've had my compensation,' said Charlie. 'Your Klaris was responsible for this and you've gotta pay. I might've been killed you know.'

'Klaris?' Flea asked. 'No it can't have been her. She doesn't know anything about bikes.'

'Course it was her,' spat Charlie. 'Who else would want to try and kill a nice boy like me?'

With super-human effort I resisted the temptation to give him a list.

'It has to be one of *them*. Everyone knows your Klaris has gone rogue, so it doesn't take much to work out who's to blame.'

There was silence for a moment, then Charlie said, 'Twenty quid, or you get what's coming to you.'

'Come on, Charlie,' I said. 'He hasn't got any money. He's only seven.'

'Empty your pockets,' he barked at Flea.

Flea felt down his sides and looked confused. 'These shorts don't have pockets, which is quite unusual. Most of my trousers do. Some have them at the sides and the back.'

One of the other boys, Jamie Khan, nodded towards me. 'What about him?'

Charlie thought for a second, then shook his head. 'No, this is between me and that thing he's keeping.' He sighed. 'So, I suppose it's gonna have to be a punishment instead.'

He turned to one of the older boys and held out his hand. My heart jumped as I saw a flash of something black and silver being handed over. It looked like a knife. Was he really going to stab Flea over a broken brake cable?

'No, Charlie,' I shouted. 'Put that away!'

But he ignored me.

'Come here,' he ordered, and Flea walked straight over, as if he was in a trance.

Charlie held the object up, which I could now see was a black marker pen, and he drew a large letter K on Flea's forehead before sending him back to me.

'That's K for killer, by the way. And now everyone will know what's hiding in your head—a killer.'

As we walked away I could hear one of them shouting, 'You keep yourselves and all that weird stuff out of the village. We don't want to end up dead in our beds because of people like you!'

We walked on in silence.

'I'm sorry,' Flea said as we approached the high street.

'It's not your fault. They're just idiots. But how did they know?'

Flea shrugged. 'Maybe Rocky. He likes them. He plays football with them sometimes.'

I wanted to disagree, to defend my best friend, to say he wouldn't betray his brother, but I knew Flea was probably right.

'I don't really mind about the K actually,' Flea said. 'Cos it's K for Klaris, isn't it? Pretty lucky really, when you think about it. I expect it'll wear off soon, and when it does I might write it on again.'

I looked at him walking along with the wonky letter on his forehead and I had to laugh.

'You really are strange, Flea. Here, take these.' I handed him the rest of his chocolate buttons and we walked home in silence.

My Weirdo

Back at the house I had something to sort out.

Rocky was lounging in front of the TV as usual. I marched up to the screen and switched it off.

'What the hell?' Rocky said, chucking a cushion at me. 'I was watching that.'

I caught the cushion and threw it back hard, aiming for his head.

'You've been talking to that village lot about Klaris, haven't you?'

He looked confused, then shrugged. 'What are you on about? Just switch my programme back on.'

'I can't believe you'd do that to Flea.'

His jaw jutted forward, ready for a fight. 'Do what? Speak to my friends?'

'Yeah!'

He smiled and shook his head. 'Joseph, you know you're getting as weird as him. What the hell's your problem?'

'Well, only that we just got ambushed by Charlie Frazer and his gang. He tried to get twenty quid off Flea because you told him Klaris has gone rogue. You should see what Frazer's done to him cos we couldn't pay up.'

Rocky's face turned a stinging red. 'So how was I supposed to know that would happen? You're acting like it's my fault. D'you think I told them to harm my own brother?'

'I don't know. You're always calling Flea a weirdo.'

'Yeah, cos he *is* a weirdo. But he's *my* weirdo, you know. If that lot have done anything to him I'll go and sort them out. But what I don't get is why you care so much.'

'Why?' The breath felt hot in my lungs and I needed to sit down. 'Because he's my friend.'

'Yeah, and it seems like nowadays you prefer spending time with a seven-year-old weirdo than with me.' He put his head in his hands for a moment. Then he spoke, his voice quiet and calm. 'I've been thinking—if you did, y'know, get coshed, would it really be so bad for you? It's not like for Flea and Klaris. You're not going to lose someone you love, are you?'

I didn't reply, just put my head down onto the arm of the sofa and stared into space.

'Whatever, Joseph,' he said, and I heard the door slam behind him.

I sat there for a minute, waiting for my heart rate to slow down. Of course Rocky wouldn't understand.

Your strongest imaginings it said.

The leaflet his dad had given me described exactly how they do it. The patient wears a cap covered in electronic probes, and has to call up the imaginary person. Often they won't come, so instead the kid's told to produce their *strongest imaginings* and think of something they long for: Christmas, a pony, a trip to the moon. The doctor studies his screen, trying to locate it—the place our creativity begins, the place where our dreams grow, the place where they live. And then . . . And then a button is pressed.

And I thought of my mum.

There, on the Cliffs' sofa, just for a minute, I gave in and let myself imagine her standing in the doorway with her suitcase and a suntan, and a look on her face that said I'm sorry, Joseph. I'm sorry I left you, and I'll never go again.

And from somewhere in the back of my mind a feeling grew. It flooded warmth through my body, radiating out through my chest.

Klaris was hugging me.

She knew I missed my mum and she was trying to comfort me, and it felt good.

Then it was over and I realized that Flea had come into the room and was sitting next to me.

'D'you want to interview the twins this afternoon?'

And instead of the idea filling me with dread, I just said, 'Yeah, bring it on.'

Like a Cat in Pain

About an hour later I was stretched out on the sofa when there was a knock at the door. I opened it and Mrs Cliff was standing there with a small boy gripped under each arm.

I leaned towards them. 'Hi Wills, hi Egg. Grrrr!'

The twins' faces were a mess of smudged orange and black tiger stripes, they had wet hair, and they were wearing large white T-shirts with We Saved the Steeple printed on the front.

'We've been to the church summer fair,' their mother explained. 'And these two lunatics volunteered to have sponges thrown at them.'

'Lucky the paints didn't get washed off,' I said.

A strange voice came from one of the orange faces.

'Not paint. Me real tiger.' He yowled like a cat in pain and scratched my arm. I tried not to react, but

Mrs Cliff saw the four angry red tracks that his nails had left behind.

'Wills, Egg, whichever one of you it was, say sorry for that!'

The boys said sorry in unison, as if they were both guilty. Their mum looked like she might grab them both and drag them back home. Unfortunately for me she didn't.

'Joseph, if it's all right with you, I'll need to leave the twins here and go back to the house for half an hour. I'm, er, I'm expecting an important work call in a few minutes.' She looked at her youngest sons, who were scanning the room with magpie expressions. 'Be good, both of you,' she said and turned and walked quickly away.

With their mum gone I knew I had to take control fast. 'OK, boys.'

'Tigers.'

'Sorry, Tigers. Did Flea tell you that I need to ask a couple of questions?'

They shook their heads from left to right. If they ever introduced synchronized lying as an Olympic sport they'd get a gold.

'Come and sit here with me so we can have a chat.' They both turned their heads towards me then, slowly, came over to the table where I'd set up my dad's old boom box. I pressed record.

JR: So, Wills and Egg, we're a bit worried about Klaris. And, well, I thought maybe we could talk about her?

Twin 1: What are all these?

JR: They're keys.

Twin 2. Why are they in here?

JR: We keep all our keys in this bowl so we don't lose them.

Twin 1: Oh.

JR: So, a few things in the house have been happening and we're wondering—

Twin 2: What's this one for?

JR: I think it's my dad's spare car key. OK, let's talk about cars. I've heard that someone's been leaving the lights on in—

Twin 2: Can we keep it?

JR: No, sorry, my dad needs it.

Twin 1: What's this one?

JR: It's for my bike lock. Hey, who's got the car key? Come on, my dad will do his nut if I lose his spare.

Twin 2: What about this tiny one? He doesn't need it; it's much too small.

JR: Yes, he does. It's for the padlock to the boat. He needs them all. So, let's put them all back. Give me the bowl please. Oh, no, now they're on the floor.

Twin 1: Here you go.

JR: Thanks. Is that all of them?

Twin 2: Yes, nearly.

JR: What about that one? Can I have it back please?

Twin 1: No.

JR: Don't do that, it's dangerous!

Twin 1: Too late.

Twin 2: Mmm, tiger food.

JR: Oh, my God! Hey, you two come back! Come back! Oh, no!

Jelly Snakes

I'd never seen anyone do something like that before. I can't even swallow a little tablet without gagging. But Wills or Egg—even their mother couldn't tell them apart in that face paint—had just popped a key into his mouth and made it disappear. I tried to tell myself that he'd hidden it under his tongue, or slipped it into his pocket, but, as I ran, my heart slamming, over to the Cliffs' house, I knew I was wrong. I knew that the key was already way beyond the reach of anyone without specialist medical equipment.

I barged through the back door and ran, two worn-carpeted steps at a time, up to the study, but it was empty.

'Mrs Cliff! Mrs Cliff!' I ran back downstairs, looking in the kitchen, living room, dining room and laundry. The place seemed deserted.

I was just running back up the stairs when I heard

the bathroom door unlock and a wall of steam and lavender hit me. I felt transported back to being eight or nine. My mum would collect fresh lavender from the garden and run it into her bath when she was feeling stressed. My dad would look anxious and tell me that Mum wasn't too well and I should leave her alone for a while.

'Oh, Joseph, my, er, my call was cancelled and I, er . . .' Looking past Mrs Cliff I could see a magazine abandoned on the wet floor and the still smoking remains of a stubbed-out cigarette in a silver ashtray.

She wrapped the belt of her white towelling dressing gown around her waist and tied it loosely. 'Is everything alright?'

I started running back downstairs shouting out behind me, 'He's swallowed a key! One of the twins has swallowed a key!'

She padded down after me in her slippers. 'Oh, the stupid boy! Which one was it?'

'I don't know. I couldn't tell them apart.'

'Where are they now?'

'Here, I think. They ran over this way.'

She reached the hallway.

'Wills! Egg! Where are you? This is important.'

Silence.

She tried to soften her voice. 'You're not going to be in trouble, I just need to talk to you.' We both knew they'd never fall for that. She changed tactics again and called for reinforcements. 'Rocky! Pooh! We need your help.'

The living-room door opened and Rocky appeared, his eyes wide and staring from too much TV. 'Hey, Joseph, wassup?' At least he'd got over our argument from earlier.

I let Mrs Cliff do the talking. 'Help us find the twins. One of them has done something stupid.'

Rocky sniggered. 'Yeah, so what's new?'

'Yes, well, this time it's something stupid *and* dangerous. So get out there and help us look for them.'

'What's going on?' Pooh was standing at the top of the stairs.

I spoke. 'It's Wills, or Egg. One of them, anyway, has swallowed a key.'

'Which key?'

'The key to the padlock for my dad's boat, I think.'

Rocky was grinning. 'There you go, Pooh, you didn't have to worry. It wasn't the key to his heart.'

Pooh hurled a fat paperback that had been lying at her feet and it hit Rocky on the back of the head.

It looked like Mrs Cliff had finally had enough because she put on her teacher's voice. 'When-you-lot have-finished-mucking-around-would-it-be-too-much-trouble-to-help-me-locate-the-twins?'

'What does locate mean?' The little voice came from just behind me. Egg's face was almost wiped clean and he was back in cut-off shorts and an old green T-shirt.

His mother grabbed him by the shoulders. 'Oh, my God, there you are. Who was it that swallowed the key? Was it you?'

He turned and looked back into the gloom of the kitchen where Wills stood, still in his tiger-striped glory, with a packet of jelly snakes in his hand. I felt in my pocket for the sweets I'd bought as a bribe for the twins.

They had gone.

Mrs Cliff went to call her husband, and came back with some bad news.

'I have to take him straight to hospital for a scan. He should, er, pass it naturally, but that could take a few days and they'll want to keep him under observation until it reappears.'

Pooh and Rocky were making sick faces and laughing, but they stopped looking quite so happy when she added, 'You two are on babysitting duty. It's a late surgery tonight, and your dad won't be back until eight. This could take a couple of days, so, until I'm home, you'll be looking after Flea and Egg while your dad's working.'

Rocky moaned, 'That's child exploitation.' But we all ignored him.

'I can help too,' I said. 'And my dad's around most of the time.'

Mrs Cliff looked relieved. 'That's very kind of you, Joseph. But I'm sure you have other things to do.'

'It's fine. I need to spend a bit of time with Egg anyway. How about I take him for a walk with me this afternoon?' I turned to Egg. 'A walk and a talk, eh?'

The expression on his face was unreadable, but I sensed fear behind the mask. I was finally in a position of power over at least one of the twins.

'That's very kind of you, Joseph. Isn't it, Egg?' said his mother. Egg ignored her. 'And, as you're going, would you mind taking the dogs along too? Here,' she handed me a bundle of little black plastic bags. 'You'll need these.'

'Er, yeah, OK.'

Annie and Henry had silently joined the meeting, like oily black shadows lurking behind us. Would I ever grow to like dogs? I doubted it. I couldn't believe they were called man's best friend. If I had a best friend who expected me to pick up his crap I'd go off him pretty quick.

'Come on, Egg,' I said. 'You call the dogs, they'll listen to you.'

Oil on a Puddle

We set off along the path that bordered the fields behind the houses. The corn reached up to Egg's shoulders and the thick stalks leaned over, scratching us as we walked. It wouldn't be long before it was cut and the spiky stubble ploughed back into the land.

They used to burn it, and my dad had told me how the rabbits and field mice would come shooting out from the flames, running in crazy circles. I knew that Egg probably felt just like those rabbits and mice, and I was sorry for him. I put my hand in my pocket, forgetting again, for an instant, that he had already stolen the treat from me. When I felt the emptiness my pity dried up.

'So, Egg. Why don't you two want to talk to me about Klaris?' He didn't respond. Even his eyes gave nothing away.

I carried on. 'They're blaming Klaris for lots of things, and they might get rid of her.'

No response.

'Flea's really upset, you know. And I'm going to help him find out what really happened.' I stopped and leant down towards him. 'So we were wondering if maybe you know something that could help us save her from the Cosh.'

I held his gaze for a moment before his eyes slipped beyond me to two figures coming through the field. Ahead of them the corn seemed to be bowing down as they walked, and I heard a low snarling which grew louder by the second.

'Tyler and Ethan Jones.' I muttered their names softly. 'What now?'

Annie reacted first. She stood rigid, the fur on her back rising into a Mohican, making her look enormous with her sagging belly below. Then Henry caught on and started growling, but he was drowned out by Digger's sudden frantic screaming bark. Egg's voice came out in a squeak. 'It's going to bite us! Run!'

But I wasn't going anywhere. The smell of Flea's humiliation was still fresh, and I wasn't about to walk away again.

Digger had finally burst through the parting stalks and stood a few metres from the Labradors, growling and weighing up his chances against two dogs bigger than himself. The seconds stretched and I thought he was going to turn and run, but, as if an invisible flag had been dropped, the three suddenly flew at each other merging at once into a dust ball of teeth, legs and tails.

Over and over they went, the dogs snarling and yelping along with our terrified shouts, and soon foamy blood-stained saliva spotted the gold and brown of Digger's fur.

In the end it was Ethan who had the good idea. He grabbed his big brother and started to run back into the corn. I thought they were leaving us to it, but then Digger looked up to see where they were going, and reluctantly followed the boys. Henry ran after him for a moment, to see him off, but soon turned around and limped back.

Annie was lying on her side panting, and he nuzzled her gently. She staggered to her feet, then bumped down again and licked her wounds.

I went over and stroked her head. 'I've never seen the dogs do anything like that before,' I said to Egg.

'It's because they knew we were in danger,' he replied. 'They were only protecting us.'

It was a miracle—the fight had shocked Egg into talking to me, and we felt like a team as me and Egg crouched down with Annie and Henry while their panting slowed and they licked the blood from their fur.

'Looks like we were lucky, Egg. I don't think they've got any serious injuries.' I stroked Annie's head again gently. 'Didn't anyone ever tell you it's unladylike to fight in your condition?' She licked my hand, and, for once, I didn't feel repulsed. I felt sort of honoured.

I wanted to go back to the house, but the dogs picked themselves up and trotted ahead as if nothing had happened, Henry pausing to sniff at clumps of grass and cock his leg, and Annie ambling behind with her belly swinging.

'Shall we do one loop round the Island, then head back?' Egg nodded. 'Shame we haven't got anything for the ducks.'

He put his hand in his pocket and pulled out a bag of Rocky's crisps.

'I didn't know ducks like crisps,' I said. 'Well, I suppose they can't be too fussy.'

That day there were just two ducks; a pair of mallards. The female, like an old farmer's wife in her tweedy browns, and the male with his emerald neck shimmering like oil on a puddle.

'Aren't they lovely, Egg? You see the pretty one with the bright colours? That's actually the boy.' He smiled. The gender politics of colour didn't mean much to him. The twins were just as happy in pink cast-offs from Pooh as in Rocky's old Action-Man khaki.

'These two are mates. It's like they're married. They'll be together for their whole lives.'

He looked beyond the ducks to the Island. 'When is Wills coming back?'

I couldn't help grinning. 'When the key reappears. Is it weird for you, being without him?'

Egg nodded.

'D'you know that if one of these two ducks goes missing, the other one will wander around everywhere looking for it? And it will never ever give up.'

'That's sad.'

'Yes.'

'Egg, that's how Flea will feel if they get rid of Klaris.'

'We want her to go.' He was sprinkling the crisps at the edge of the water and the ducks were spooning them like croutons in their plasticky beaks. 'Flea just got her so he could have a special person.'

'A special person? You mean, like you and Wills?'

'Yes, and Rocky and you, and Pooh and her friend Emily from school. Flea didn't have an anyone, so he got one. But she's just imaginary. And we don't like imaginary people.'

'But wouldn't it be sad if Flea lost his friend?'

He shrugged.

'Egg, why don't you and Wills like Klaris?'

'She's mean. She made Flea tell on us when we did stuff.'

'What sort of stuff?'

'Once, when we made a magic potion and put it in Rocky's Coke bottle, Klaris made Flea tell mum.'

I smiled. The twins' concoctions were legendary. 'And what was in the potion?'

'Plant food and parrots eat 'em all.'

'What parrots?'

'No, the headache pills that mum always takes after she shouts at us.'

'Ah, you mean paracetamol. Did he drink it?'

'Only a bit.'

'And what happened?'

'He said it tasted nice. But Mum said it was dangerous and shouted at Dad because he hadn't put a lock on the medicine cabinet. And Dad shouted at Mum and called us bloody, and then they just argued with each other.'

Egg shook the last bits of crisp out of the packet.

'If I lost Wills I would wander the whole world, the whole universe, the whole everything until I found him.'

'I hope you never have to, Egg,' I said. 'Losing someone you love isn't much fun.'

THURSDAY

At Your Age

One day to go and I was feeling seriously anxious. We had to hurry up and get the evidence to Dr Cliff so he could cancel the RIPS appointment. But we just weren't ready.

In the movies when a hero's scared he has a nerve twitching in his jaw. My nerves were showing themselves in diarrhoea and sweaty armpits. There was no relief from it at night either. My dreams were full of men in white coats chasing me with swimming caps and twelve-volt batteries.

I wanted to tell my dad, but I'd left it too late. What was the point now? He'd only freak out. If it all went wrong he'd find out anyway. They could hardly give me the Cosh without his permission.

Besides, he had his own worries.

'Tell me something, Joseph—and I want you to be honest—do you think I'm too old for this shirt?'

'No, probably not.'

'What goes best: trainers, or smart shoes?'

'Whatever you think, Dad, both look fine.'

'Shall I shave just before I go out and risk cutting myself? Or should I shave in the morning and go for the rugged five-o'clock shadow?'

'Er, midday?'

'You don't think she'll want to go clubbing afterwards, do you?'

'Yes, I'm sure she will.'

That's the danger with not listening properly.

He sunk into the chair, and his face seemed to slide half an inch down the front of his skull.

'Really? Well, p'raps I'd better text her and cancel.'

I thought for a second. Did I want him to cancel his date? Yes, probably. I didn't want my dad starting out on a 'new phase', as he put it. I wanted the old phase back, with me and Mum and Dad living happily ever after.

But with RIPS coming I needed my dad out of the way.

'Why d'you want to cancel?'

'Oh, you know clubbing's not really my thing. I can just about look half decent if I'm stationary. Once I start moving I've blown it. I'd rather stay at home with you and not risk making an idiot of myself.'

It was time for some reverse psychology.

'Yeah, I think you're right, Dad. You'd be much

better off here. I mean, I'm not being rude, but being a stay-at-home kind of bloke suits you. Which isn't a bad thing, is it? It stands to reason not everyone can lead an exciting life, or all the nightclubs would be full, and they'd have to grow more grapes for extra bottles of champagne and build loads more private jets, and that would be bad for the environment and all that.'

He looked up. 'So, you're saying that I ought to be boring for the sake of the environment? Joseph, I don't know what you're implying about me. I voted Green at the last election, but I still know how to have a good time.'

I smiled. 'Course I'm not saying you ought to be boring. It's just that maybe you shouldn't overdo things at your age.'

'Joseph, I'm forty-four not eighty-four! I've got more stamina than a lot of twenty-year olds. Here, I'll give you a kick around in the garden. I'll show you who's past it!'

He went to the under-stairs cupboard and I heard him fighting with the Hoover and chucking roller blades and football boots behind him as he worked his way back towards the ball. Then there was a dull thud as he cracked his head on the underside of the stair above him, followed by some pretty loud Class A swearing. He came out rubbing his scalp, with a deflated football in his hand.

He threw it at me. 'Here, take this next door and

borrow a pump, will you? And I'll get the picnic stuff out and do us some squash and biscuits for after. Now, where is that basket? Haven't seen it for ages. And the picnic rug too. Have you taken them next door and left them there?'

'Nope.'

'You sure? That's weird. Where else could I have put them?' He stuck his head back into the cupboard. 'They must be in the back here somewhere.'

'You know what, Dad, I'd rather do something else.'

He pulled his head out, looking upset. 'Why? You love footie. We could get the others involved, have a big match.'

'Yeah. Another time maybe, just not today. I feel like staying inside.' I chucked the ball into the gloom of the cupboard again.

'OK, fair enough. I should think you're saving your strength for going back to school.'

'Yeah, that's probably it.'

'And you've been helping Flea, haven't you?' He started piling the boots back into the cupboard. 'I meant to ask, how's it going?'

'OK, I suppose.'

'Y'know I was thinking about that. It's strange that Dr C's so down on Klaris, what with him having had one too.'

I froze. 'Dr Cliff used to have an imaginary person? Are you sure about that?'

'Yeah. Now what was it he told me one Christmas after a few too many sherries? Howard, Horace? He called it something like that, I'm sure. Sounded very fond of him. Got a bit teary just talking about it actually.'

Yeah, she's working from home today. But be careful,
he's in an even worse mood than usual. Going on about
someone taking his Dictaphone. I expect that's on the
Klaris list by now.

The S Word

I bumped into Pooh in the hallway next door.

'Rocky's in his room,' she said.

'Actually I need a word with your dad. Is he here?'

She did that eyebrow thing again.

'Yeah, he's working from home today. But be careful,
he's in an even worse mood than usual. Going on about
someone taking his Dictaphone. I expect that's on the
Klaris list by now.'

'Didn't you tell him you broke it?'

She laughed. 'As if.'

I went upstairs to where Dr Cliff was doing telephone
consultations. I could hear his booming voice through
the heavy study door.

'Yes ... Yes ... Hmm ... Yes ... Hmm ... Yes, I think
that might be the best course of action for the moment.
OK, cheerio.'

Being a doctor sounded pretty easy.

I knocked on the door and heard a bad-tempered, 'What is it?' His voice softened when I entered, and he adjusted his glasses, pushing his wispy grey baby hair over his pink bald patch.

'Joseph? What can I do for you? Are you looking for Rocky? I've sent him out to walk Henry.' He looked down at Annie who seemed to be asleep on his feet. 'She's too tired and fat to do much at the moment, poor thing.'

I wondered if he knew that she had been scrapping with a Staffie the day before, but decided not to mention it.

'Actually it's you I need to speak to.'

'Ah, I see.' He leaned back in his creaky brown-leather chair with his hands clasped behind his head. 'Read the leaflet I gave you, hmm?'

'Yes.'

'Excellent, my boy. So, I expect you've got a question. Ask away. Anything at all.'

'Yes, I have got a question. It's about . . . Well, it's about *your* imaginary person. The one you had when you were young.'

He jolted upright. 'Mine? Well, well . . .' He licked his lips. 'I'm not sure that's entirely relevant to this situation.'

'What I was wondering is, how can you do this to Klaris when you had one yourself?'

His flabby jowls pinked and wobbled as he banged

his fist on the desk. 'It's precisely *because* I had one myself that I'm doing this. Because I know the damage they can cause.'

'I don't understand.'

'No, of course you don't. How could you? You haven't lived through it. Now, I'm very busy, so if you wouldn't mind . . .'

I stood my ground. 'Can't you tell me so I *will* understand? What was his name?'

Dr Cliff sighed and stared beyond me, out through the window. 'Horatio.' He smiled thinly at the memory. 'I remember it all so well. He got in when my brother started school.' He looked directly at me. 'Played by myself too much, I suppose. But, you see, they didn't know any better in those days. They were different times. Innocent times. We didn't know the dangers. Didn't know what to look for. It all changed, of course, after Shorefield.'

Shorefield. The S word. You just had to say it and anything was allowed. Even frying a kid's brain.

Dr Cliff looked out of the window again, and when he spoke his voice was raspy.

'And now history's repeating itself.'

'No, it's not. Klaris is just a normal, boring imaginary person. She hasn't done anything wrong.'

He snorted. 'You can't see the damage a rogue does to a family until it's too late. My poor parents certainly didn't see it coming. They thought he was just a useful amusement for a lonely child. And he was, for a while. Best friend I ever had in fact. But then . . .' He took off his glasses and rubbed his bloodshot eyes. 'Then one day my mother left us and my father remarried and I was packed off to boarding school. I was only seven. The same age as Flea is now.' He put his glasses back on. 'I'm not going to risk the same thing happening to this family.'

'But lots of parents split up. You can't blame your imaginary person for that.'

He glared at me and almost spat out the words. 'My mother loved me. She loved us all. She would never have left unless someone or something made her.'

He took a crumpled hankie from his pocket and blew his nose.

'Dr Cliff, this isn't Shorefield. And Klaris isn't Horatio. She's innocent, and we're gathering the evidence to prove it to you. We've got loads already. If you stay here I'll go and fetch my notes. Then will you please cancel the RIPS visit? You could say you've changed your mind, or you made a mistake. Or say we played a trick on you.'

He looked down at the silver-framed photograph on his desk. It was Mrs Cliff in a long white wedding dress, laughing and with confetti in her dark hair. Beside her was a tall, slim man with blond curls poking out from beneath a top hat, and a huge grin just like Rocky's. It took me a moment to realize that it was Dr Cliff, about a million years ago.

When he spoke his voice was brisk, business-like again. 'I'm sorry, Joseph, but I can't do that. We have to follow the official advice. A potential rogue must be reported and, if necessary, removed before they can do real harm.'

'But you're wrong about her! And we've got evidence!'

He shook his head.

'And what about me and Flea? D'you actually *want* us to have the Cosh?'

'What I want is irrelevant, Joseph. It's out of my hands. No matter what I say now, RIPS will send someone over tomorrow to do the necessary diagnostic tests, weigh up the evidence, ascertain whether or not Klaris is a danger, and plan the relevant course of action.' He tried to do his reassuring doctor's smile. 'You don't need to worry though, they're highly skilled professionals and they won't carry out any medical procedure unless it's absolutely necessary.'

I got up to leave. As I reached for the door he spoke again.

'I'd appreciate it if you didn't share what we've discussed with Flea. I'm doing what's best for everyone,' he said. 'When it's all over you'll thank me, you'll see.'

Break Your Heart

My dad was sitting on the back step, the contents of the shoe-cleaning basket strewn around him.

'Here,' he threw the whitening cream at me. 'You can do your trainers. They're a bit old, but we bought them big, and they should clean up OK. I've already done your school shoes.'

'They didn't need cleaning. They're new.'

'Now that's where you're wrong, Joseph. Shoes are often thirsty when you first get them.'

'Thirsty?'

'Well, not literally, of course. But they do need a good feed with a bit of polish so they don't crack the first time you get them wet. Don't forget the summer's nearly over. You'll soon be walking to school in the rain again.'

'It doesn't seem possible, does it?' I said. 'Remember when it snowed last year? We had loads of layers on, and hats and gloves, and we were still so cold it hurt.'

'And now we're sitting here sweating in just our shorts. So we should make the most of it because the weather'll turn soon enough.'

The idea came to me as I squeezed an inch of white cream onto the scuffed toes of my trainer. I looked up, excited. 'Not if we go to Spain, Dad. It's always warm there.'

'Depends which part you're in. The north's quite cold in the winter. You can even ski there, you know, up in the mountains.'

'Please can we just go, Dad? There's a week left of my holidays. We could get a cheap flight, leave tonight. We could try and find Mum.'

He jumped up. 'Here, careful! You'll get it all over your clothes.'

He handed me a rag and I wiped the cream, now dripping like milk, off the sole of my trainer.

'It's gone a bit runny in the heat,' he said. 'We should've done this inside really, but I wanted to get a bit of a tan.'

'You're ignoring my question, Dad. Why can't we just go?'

He sighed. 'Because she might not . . . She might . . .' He looked pained as he rubbed the back of his neck. 'Look, Spain's a big country, Joseph. We could be searching for ever.'

'So? We've got for ever, haven't we?'

My words hung in the air for a moment, but my dad didn't reply. I should've known he wouldn't agree. It was hopeless. I was going to have to face RIPS, and there was nothing I could do to change it.

I finished whitewashing the first trainer and put it down to dry. It looked a mess, like an albatross had just relieved itself on my foot.

'I spoke to Flea's dad just now,' I said.

'Oh, yeah? Did you persuade him to leave Klaris alone?'

'No. It's too late for that. Some person from RIPS is coming tomorrow.'

My dad stopped polishing and shook his head. 'Oh, that's bad news. Poor little Flea. Poor Klaris. I can't believe it.'

He seemed really upset. And that was before he knew that *my* brain was next in line for the Cosh.

'I can't believe it's come to this. Institutionalized murder, I call it.' He gave the toe of his shoe a hard rub. 'The nonsense they talk nowadays you'd think they were public enemy number one instead of a bit of company for a lonely kid. I've got a good mind to go over and have a word with Dr C. It's not right.'

'No!' I tried to sound casual, but failed. 'No, he's busy with patients. He's in a bad mood anyway, and he'll be really annoyed if you disturb him.'

My dad looked unconvinced, but carried on cleaning.

'I've been reading up about it online, Joseph, and

there's people out there who're pressurizing the government over Shorefield; they're called the Defence for Imaginary People, or something like that. Anyway they're trying to get the investigation reviewed.'

He rubbed the shoe until it shone. 'Cos a lot of people think it was a cover up.' He sighed. 'Anyway, whatever happens it'll be too late for little Flea. Y'know I think it's come to something when grown men are trying to destroy a kid's imagination. It shouldn't be allowed.' He put the lid back on the polish tin and forced a smile. 'But I suppose no one should be allowed to knock your confidence, or shatter your hopes, or break your heart either. And they frequently do.'

I looked through the open door to my mum's postcard, which was still sitting propped up against her old novels.

'Did Mum break your heart, Dad?'

He smiled. 'No, Joseph, but she took it off me, slapped it into shape, and gave it back so I'd be able to look after you.' He grinned. 'If they do a post-mortem when I die they'll find her initials, CR, burned right through it like a brand on a cow's hide.'

I winced at the image. 'But what about this date tomorrow, Dad? I mean, where does that leave you and Mum?'

He heaved another sigh, this one so big that I saw his body rise and fall, then he put his hand gently on my arm.

'Joseph, your mum is the love of my life. And if she was here it would be different. But she's not, and p'raps it's time for us to get on with living. We both need to. We can't keep on acting as though she's going to walk back through the door at any moment. It's been too long since we heard anything from her.'

My throat felt tight, and my voice was high. 'It's only been two years and a few months, Dad. That's not long. She sent that postcard just before I was eleven, remember? She said she'd be back soon.'

He sniffed and searched in his pocket for a tissue. 'Can we leave it for today, eh?'

'OK.' I picked up my trainers. 'I'll take these inside to finish them off. I'm getting a bit hot out here.'

'Fair enough. But make sure you put some newspaper down on the table first.'

Inside the house felt as cool as a cave. I spread out a couple of sheets from the local free paper, and dumped the shoe cleaning stuff on top of the car ads. Then I decided the trainers could wait.

I went over to the shelf, checked my hands and wiped a smear of white stuff from under my thumbnail onto my T-shirt. Then I took down the Scottish shortbread tin and opened it.

Eight altogether, if you counted the most recent one that was still sitting on the shelf. The first three were written soon after she arrived, in the spring, and they were different. More informative, more jokey. And she mentioned her sister, who was travelling with her.

Lois and me bought sombreros today—you should see us—we look like total idiots!

The waiter was chatting Lois up this evening. He was a dead ringer for Pavarotti!

Lois used her best Spanish to ask directions to the hotel, and we ended up at the Town Hall!

And she said how she was feeling.

Just lying on the hot sand listening to the waves is so relaxing.

I'm beginning to feel like a different person.

I think they should bottle Spain and sell it at the chemist's. It's working for me!

And, of course, that she missed me.

Oh, Joseph, if only you were here too this place would be paradise!

I'm longing to see you.

I just so want to show you all of this.

So, why the hell didn't she?

I didn't bother to look at the last four postcards. They came after a break of a few weeks. By then Mum and her sister had split up. Lois had fallen in love with a wind-surfing instructor called Pablo in Marbella, and my mum had slipped into one of her moods and set off on her own. They were short notes, and she was starting to sound distant, uncertain, lonely. Like she used to be on her worst days, when I would try to talk to her, but she'd just cry

150

or stare out of the window, or worse, look straight through me.

And then, after another gap when we'd just started to worry about her, the last postcard came.

I took it down off the shelf and turned it over.

Guess what, Joseph? I'll be back with you in the summer—so keep your eyes open, you never know when it will be!!!!

She'd said she was coming home.

Only she didn't.

I hadn't noticed Flea by the door. He did his little knock thing again.

'Is it OK to come in?'

I wiped the tear from my eye with the back of my hand.

'Yeah. We need to talk anyway.'

His forehead looked different.

'Hey, your K's gone green.'

'Yes. It had faded so I did it again with Pooh's oil paints. D'you like it?'

'Er, yeah, it's . . . individual.'

He sat down on the chair next to me and picked up the pile of postcards. I had to resist the temptation to snatch them from him.

'Are these from your mum?'

I nodded, my eyes fixed on the precious cards. I relaxed as he put them carefully back inside the tin.

'To be honest I'm worried, Flea. We've only got one

more day, and we still haven't finished the list. I've spoken to your dad and he's refusing to even hear our evidence.'

He shrugged. 'It'll be OK. We'll just tell the RIPS person himself when he comes.'

'Yeah, it's our only option. But it's risky. And what if we don't find all the answers?'

'You still need to speak to my mum. She usually knows everything that's going on.'

'Is she back from the hospital?'

'Not yet. But she will be as soon as Wills poos out the key. Perhaps he's on the loo right now and she'll come home tonight.'

'Well, I hope so, Flea. Because I can't just point at some random member of your family and accuse them of framing Klaris. I still have to live next door, and see them every day. I can't get it wrong.'

Very Buddhist

Flea had to go and help look after Egg, so I finished cleaning my trainers then wandered outside. I found Henry lying in the shade of the old vines that snaked up the Cliffs' back wall and dripped with bunches of purple flowers like grapes. I knelt down and stroked his head, resisting the urge to wipe my hand on my trousers afterwards. His tail wagged lazily, raising dust on the dry ground.

'Do you know what happened, boy? D'you know who did all that stuff?' His tail kept up its metronome beat, and I sighed and went to stand.

'Caught ya!' It was Rocky. 'Finally cracked up, eh?'

'Yeah, possibly.'

'Not finished the investigation yet?'

I shook my head.

Rocky snorted. 'Must be fascinating. More interesting than hanging out with me anyway.'

So I wasn't forgiven after all.

'From this Friday I'm all yours, I promise. As long as my brain isn't too crispy to keep up with your sparkling conversation.'

'But that's practically the end of the holidays,' he whined. 'Weekends don't count cos we get them anyway. Can't you have a day off? Come into town with me. I have to visit my mum and stupid key-swallowing brother at the hospital, but that won't take long, and then we can go and have some fun.'

'OK, but what about Egg? Aren't you supposed to be looking after him while your dad's at work?'

'Yeah, I'm on duty this morning, and Pooh's doing this afternoon.'

'So where is he?'

Rocky shrugged. 'I dunno. I told Flea to play with him. 'They're probably out here somewhere.' We scanned the garden and listened for their voices. The only sound was a nearby gunshot.

'Pigeon murderers,' he said.

'Oh, don't go all vegetarian on me, Rocky. You eat meat.'

'Yeah, but I don't kill things for sport. That's just sick.'

He flicked a fly that had landed on his chest. 'Die, you evil vomit-eating pest!'

I raised my eyebrows. 'Very Buddhist.'

'What? They eat their own sick. It's a fact.' Then, in

a weary shout, 'Fle-ea! E-egg! Biscuits in the kit-chen.'

We wandered over to the house in a silence that was only broken by the sound of Rocky's flip-flops as he walked, and the occasional pop from a distant rifle. Egg had beaten us to the kitchen, and was sitting on the table dissecting a Jammy Dodger.

'Hey, Egg,' I said, 'Where's Flea? Weren't you two hanging out together?'

He shook his head and crumbs flew from where they had sheltered at the corners of his mouth.

'Well, have you seen him?' He shook his head again, this time less convincingly. I felt a slight unease in my stomach, just a gentle squeeze. If I'd had the idea of going to Spain to avoid the RIPS visit, wouldn't Flea think of running away too?

'What, you haven't seen him at all? He came over to find you about half an hour ago.'

Egg shook his head again, but his eyes were fixed on his biscuit. He turned to Rocky. 'Milk, please.'

So, he hadn't lost his voice. 'Egg, tell me where Flea is.' He shrugged and stuffed the jammy disk that he had saved until last into his mouth.

I ran out, calling for Flea, but there was no reply. I tried the living room, dining room, and his bedroom. Again, nothing. Finally, I went outside and, while I was frantically scanning the whole area, I spotted a figure at the open attic window. I ran back inside and up to the third floor where, in a dusty storeroom, with boxes and furniture draped in white sheets like ghosts, I found him, leaning out of the dormer window. He didn't turn around, and I could see the spikes of his shoulder blades through his thin green T-shirt, like folded wings.

'Flea, there you are!'

He didn't reply for a moment, just went up on the balls of his feet as if he might fly out of the window.

Then he turned around, frowning. 'It's been bothering me. I know she's not a rogue, and she's not migrating in the usual sense. So why did Klaris go into you, Joseph?'

I sighed. 'I don't know, Flea. I guess I'm just lucky.'

'Yes, you are.'

'I was joking.'

'Oh.'

'Egg thinks it's my fault.'

'Egg? What's he been saying to you?'

He was silent for a moment. 'He says it's cos I'm a loser and even Klaris knows it. I think he's angry with me because of Wills.'

'Yeah, I expect so. They're not used to being apart. It must be hard for him.'

'It's not only Egg. I tried to talk to Pooh about it, but she's just worried about her school friends finding out. And Rocky thinks I'm an idiot anyway. And my dad—well, he's the one who's trying to kill her.'

I couldn't really argue with any of that. I loved his

family, but he deserved better. It's lonely being an only child, but at that moment I understood that being lonely in a crowd is even worse.

'Look, Flea, I don't know why she came to me. Believe me, I didn't encourage her. Well, not on purpose. Too much daydreaming I suppose. I . . . I think about my mum sometimes. Well, quite a lot really. Make stuff up about her coming home. Y'know, imagine her pulling up in a taxi with a big straw hat on her head and a stuffed donkey over her shoulders, that sort of thing.'

'Oh,' he said. 'That must feel nice.'

'Yeah. But the point is Klaris came to you first because you're special. You're the one with the big imagination. And you feel stuff that no one else does. Or if they do they're too embarrassed to admit it. You look and you listen and you notice things. And you're brave. Braver than all those kids at the park with their big muscles.' I sighed. 'Braver than me because I haven't even told my dad about any of this.'

Flea shrugged. 'Maybe.'

I put my arm around his bony shoulders. 'We'll save Klaris somehow. But right now I'm going down to the hospital to pay your mum and Wills a visit.'

Don't Need to Say Goodbye

Back downstairs I found Rocky filling his pockets with biscuits for the journey. 'Come on', he said, 'my babysitting duties are over for the day. So let's get out of here.'

As we passed my house, I ran in and grabbed a few things. Then we jogged up to the bus stop and got there just as the number 49 arrived.

We paid the driver, and I flashed my ID card in case he thought I was over fourteen (there's always a first time) and we headed for the back seat. I really hoped that no one big and tough would get on at the next stop and make us move. But no one else got on at all, so, ignoring the dirty looks from the driver in the mirror, Rocky kept me amused with his very loud parodies of songs, replacing the words, when he didn't know them, with farting noises. It sounds stupid, but somehow it was the funniest thing I'd ever heard. Well, I hadn't had much to laugh about for a while.

The hospital's easy to find—just a short walk from the bus stop. But once we got inside we managed to get hopelessly lost pretty much straight away.

We knew that Wills was on a children's ward called Featherdown, but it's an old hospital, with lots of different buildings linked by tunnels and bridged corridors. We tried to follow the map, but we must have gone badly wrong somewhere because we ended up in the waiting room for the Neuropathology Department instead. We'd just decided to turn round and retrace our steps when Rocky nudged me and pointed to a large sign on the wall.

OUTPATIENTS ATTENDING FOR DEPRESSION/PSYCHOSIS/IMAGINARY PERSON REMOVAL PLEASE REPORT TO THE DESK

The seating area was empty apart from a middle-aged woman, gripping a blonde child of about three tightly to her lap. The little girl had her hands over her ears and was listening and talking in a high-pitched tone. Then she looked confused.

'Don't be silly,' she said. 'We don't need to say goodbye.'

We hurried on past.

Wills looked up as we finally walked into his cubicle. He smiled at Rocky, but when he saw me he scowled and pulled the covers over his head. Fortunately his mum didn't seem to notice.

'Hello you two,' she said. It was odd to see her away from the Cliffs' kitchen. I was used to her pink-cheeked and stressed, in her plain work clothes, or a scruffy tracksuit, with her long black hair tied in a band. But that day, away from home and work, she looked relaxed and younger somehow. She smiled. 'This is a nice surprise, isn't it, Wills?'

He pulled the covers back, but still looked wary. 'Did you bring me anything?'

I reached into my bag. 'Here you go. I've brought you my DSi. Thought you might be bored.'

Wills smiled and his dark eyes widened.

His mum put her arm around me. 'Oh, Joseph, you are thoughtful. It's so boring for poor old Wills in here. I must say we've been feeling a bit ignored. They've just popped him into bed and told us to ring the bell if he's in severe pain. They haven't even x-rayed him yet—apparently they've been too busy with all the fractures from children falling off trampolines.'

She looked at her watch. 'I hate to do this to you when you've just arrived, but I have to go and make a phone call. Do you two mind keeping Wills company for a few minutes?'

Rocky looked like he was going to refuse, so I spoke

up. 'Course not. We don't mind at all, do we?'

Wills started to cry.

'What's the matter, darling? Does your tummy hurt?' His mum looked worried, but she checked her watch again. 'Look, I'll only be gone a few minutes. If it still hurts when I get back we'll call the nurse. OK?'

I had very little time, so, as she left I held a fiver out to Rocky.

'Why don't you go and buy some sweets? I'll look after Wills while you're away.'

Wills looked even more alarmed, but Rocky snatched the note and ran out.

So now it was just me and him. He clutched the DSi in his small hands and kept his gaze fixed on the door.

'It won't be much fun without a game in it, will it?' I said.

He turned the console round and saw the empty slot.

'Come on, just a quick chat then I'll give you the game as well. I need to talk to you about something that happened on Monday evening. Something that got blamed on Klaris.'

He stared at me, his eyes huge like the deer's in the road, darting from my face to the game.

'We didn't do it. It was Klaris.'

'What are you talking about?'

'The writing on the shed. It was her. It even says it was.'

I got my notebook from my bag. 'OK. I believe you.

161

But you still have to do something if you want the game. Just write her name down there and you'll get it.'

He looked suspicious, but took the pen and wrote, in wobbly letters:

CLARIS

It was spelt with a C, just like the carving on the shed.

I pointed to a dotted line I'd drawn just below it.

'Now can you show me how you write your name there?'

He paused, but I took a game out of my bag and held it just out of his reach. Then he wrote the names he and Egg practised in school:

William and Edgar Cliff

'So you can write.'

He shook his head. 'Now give me the game.'

'Here,' I said, and chucked it onto the bed covers.

Rocky appeared at the door with a carrier bag full of chocolate and crisps, and his mum came in just behind him.

'Come on,' said Rocky, 'Time to go.'

'So soon, boys?' His mum looked disappointed. 'Oh, well. It was nice of you to visit, wasn't it, Wills?'

But Wills had his head under the covers again.

'Don't worry,' I said. 'I always have that effect on

people. But before I go d'you think I could have a quick chat with you?'

'With me? Oh, well, yes, I suppose so.'

Wills started to cry again, but Mrs Cliff kissed his forehead lightly and stood up. 'Don't be silly, Wills, just call the nurse with your special button if you need anything. Come on, Joseph. I'm desperate for a proper cup of coffee.'

'I need to nip into the gaming shop,' Rocky whispered to me as we left the room. 'I've got some of Flea's old stuff to swap. See you back at the bus stop in an hour.'

Crunchy Little Saucers

At the hospital canteen I let Mrs Cliff buy me a Coke and some carrot cake, and we took a table on the terrace outside.

She pulled a packet of cigarettes from her bag, lit one and inhaled deeply, a look of satisfaction on her face. Seconds later a large lady in a blue gingham apron strode over.

'Strictly not allowed on the premises. Even out here.' She pointed to a large No Smoking sign. 'This is a hospital, you know.'

'Oh.' Mrs Cliff looked fondly at the cigarette, took a last drag and stubbed it out on an old foil container.

'So, no sign of the key yet?' I asked.

'No. Actually they're finally going to x-ray him this afternoon. I'm beginning to wonder if he made it all up; spat it out after he left your house or something. He's been acting a bit odd.' She smiled.

'Even odder than usual. And he's missing Egg terribly.'

I tried the carrot cake. It tasted like sponge—the sort you wash with.

'Anyway,' she said. 'I don't want to leave him for too long, so shall we get on with it?'

I nodded. 'The person from RIPS is coming tomorrow and there are a few things I need to know.'

She looked worried. 'Tomorrow? No one told me it would be so soon. I'm sorry. I tried to talk my husband out of it, but he's adamant. He believes that Klaris could be dangerous and we need to act.'

She ran her hands through her hair. 'He doesn't want to do it, Joseph. But he feels he has no choice. Apart from the obvious worries about our safety, he's the village doctor. If word got out that we're harbouring a rogue no one would trust him any more. His career would be over. We'd have to leave the house, leave the village even. The children would have to go to new schools and make new friends.'

'But she's not going rogue. There are simple explanations for most of the things he says she's done.'

'Good.' She pushed her coffee away and studied my face for a moment. 'OK, look, I don't want to go behind my husband's back, but if I can help in any way I will.'

'Thanks. I just need you to tell me anything about Klaris that might be useful.'

'Well, I don't really know much. I remember that

she arrived when Flea was about five. He'd had others, but they didn't stay very long.' She shook her head. 'Klaris was always different. A bit bossy, a bit moody you might say. But he never minded. In fact he's always adored her. He certainly takes more notice of her than he does of me or his father.'

She stopped to sip her coffee.

'So she's always been a good influence on him?'

Mrs Cliff nodded. 'Yes, though they've had their arguments. She can be quite interfering. And not just with Flea, with the rest of the family too.'

'Including you?'

She laughed. 'Especially me, I think.'

'What does she do?'

'Well, she hates me smoking. Flea never used to mention it until Klaris took an interest. Now it's a bit of an obsession with him, and I have to sneak around in my own home every time I want a quick puff.'

'Anything else?'

'Yes, Klaris likes to interfere in my cooking. A few weeks ago I was getting the Sunday dinner ready and Flea came in and passed on a message that if I didn't turn the oven right up my Yorkshire puddings wouldn't rise.'

'And was she right?'

'Yes, annoyingly, she was. I refused to change the oven temperature and they came out like crunchy little saucers.'

'So, you must be glad that Klaris is going.'

She paused. 'No. Well, not like this anyway. Yes, there have been times when I wished that Klaris would disappear and Flea would get some real friends. But no, I didn't want . . .' She dabbed her eyes with a napkin.

'Just a couple more things.' I took a swig of my Coke. 'About the smoking. When you say you have to sneak around your own home, where exactly do you do it?'

'Oh, out of windows, in the garden. Often in the evenings I'll sit in the car with the radio on.'

'In the dark?'

'Well, if it's dark I usually put the little interior light on. Makes it quite cosy. Why?'

'Oh, nothing really.' I ate the remains of my carrot cake, pushed my chair back and stood up. 'Thanks, you've been very helpful.'

'Really?' She smoothed down her hair and smiled. 'Well, I'm glad.'

On the way out of the hospital I went through the Neuropathology Department again. This time the waiting room was empty, and I was going to walk past. I wanted to walk past, but I didn't. Instead I went up to the heavy double doors that led into the treatment room. There were glass panels in the top half, reinforced with wire. I pushed at them, but they were locked. So I stood with my face resting against the glass and looked through.

The room was decorated in that 'cheerful' style they think will make kids forget that they're scared or in pain, or dying, with grinning clowns stencilled onto the walls, and clouds floating by on the ceiling.

Lying on a treatment table was a little boy of about four. He was wearing a green hospital gown and a multi-coloured cap, covered in electrodes. A man in a white coat, with shiny shoes and a bristly ginger goatee beard was leaning over the boy, his head angled to one side. Through the door I could just about hear the doctor's low voice.

'Come on now, I know you can do better than that. Just talk to him in your head, like you usually do, and it'll be over in no time. You might even get a lolly.' And all the while the doctor was looking between the boy's face and the computer screen showing his brain activity. 'Come on,' he said, sounding less patient, 'come on little, er,' he looked at his notes, 'little Toddy Snowflake, show yourself, we haven't got all day.'

I could see the boy's face. He was staring straight ahead, and his fingers were gripping the fabric of the gown. He made no sound but tears were rolling down and dripping onto the vinyl of the chair.

Suddenly the doctor noticed a change on his screen.

'Aha, gotcha!' he said, 'Just where I thought you'd be hiding,' and he pushed a button.

I turned quickly, and walked away, wiping my own stupid tears from my face.

FRIDAY

It's Not Over Yet

My dad was arranging flowers in a vase. Well, maybe arranging isn't the right word, but the stems all ended up in the water, and I think that's what counts.

'Look at that—drooping already,' he said, raising an orange head, which flopped straight back down again. 'Mind you I feel a bit like that too. Hottest day of the year, they're saying. Rain by tonight. So that'll be the end of the summer I expect.' He stood back to admire the effect. It wasn't great.

'They're called gerberas,' he said, now trying to turn all the wilting heads to face the same direction. 'Also known as oversized, overpriced daisies. But they were your mum's favourite. She had them in a bouquet at our wedding. She put one in my buttonhole too.' He brought the vase up to his face and sniffed, then frowned. 'I feel a bit odd today. Fluttery inside.'

'Maybe you'd better cancel tonight.'

'D'you think so?'

I walked over to the sink and poured myself a glass of water. 'I was being sarcastic. You just need to relax. I'll bet she—what's her name again?'

'Er. Milly. No, that's not right. Oh, God, I can't remember her name! Er . . . Mandy! That's right, it's Mandy.' His eyebrows drew together forcing his forehead into a hill-shaped furrow. 'What if I forget her name tonight?' He put his face in his hands. 'I can't believe it. How many women have I been out with in the last few years?'

'None.'

'Exactly! So how come I can't remember her name? And, more to the point, what will it look like if I forget it tonight?'

'You won't, Dad.'

'She'll think I'm a womanizer. She'll think I go out on dates all the time. A different one every week. Every night even!'

I sat beside him and put my hand on his shoulder. 'I doubt it, Dad. And even if it crosses her mind, it doesn't really matter. Cos after ten minutes she'll see through the nervousness to the real you.'

'D'you think so?'

'Yeah. She'll soon realize you're not a womanizer, you're just having a senior moment. It happens at your age.'

'Oi!'

'But as long as you don't let her see your incontinence pants you'll be all right.'

'Hey, you cheeky little——!'

He got up from the table, grabbed the pan scrubber from the sink, and a trail of soapy liquid started dripping onto the kitchen floor.

I didn't want an extreme exfoliating treatment, so I ran out of the back door, followed closely by a flying sponge.

'Missed!' I picked up the sponge and threw it back. It thumped wetly against the door as he slammed it just in time.

He opened the window. 'It's not over yet, Joseph!'

'Yeah, in your dreams!'

I ran round the corner, unsure where to go. I knew that if I went into the garden one of the Cliff kids would come out to join me, but what I really needed was time alone to prepare myself for what was coming. So I stayed next to the house and squatted with my back against the cool roughness of the pale pink wall and tried to think.

Dr Cliff didn't want to hear the truth, no matter how convincing it was. So we needed to find a way to present it to the person coming from RIPS, whether Dr Cliff liked it or not.

I started mentally going through the list, worried we'd forgotten something, 'Car lights—check. Stethoscope—check—'

'Joseph, run!'

It was Flea shouting from the window as my dad came lumbering round the corner, bumping a big yellow bucket along behind him. As he got close he swung it by the handle in my direction, but the bucket was too heavy, and, as it moved away from him, the water flew upwards, cascading over the edge, missing me by inches but covering my dad in cold soapy suds.

Looking over towards the garden I saw Flea and Egg pointing and laughing. I realized it was the first time I'd seen them both looking happy at the same time.

I ran into their house, leaving my dad staring down at his socks, soaked through his old Birkenstock sandals.

Flea followed me back in. 'That was really funny. Will you get him back?'

'Maybe.'

'Good. I could help you. Anyway, you're staying here tonight, so we could think something up then.'

'Yeah, but I'll be sleeping with Rocky in his stinking pit of a room.'

He put his head to one side. 'You could sleep with me and Egg if you like. Wills's bed's free.'

I paused. 'Thanks, Flea, but I think I'll put up with Rocky.'

As if on cue the boy himself appeared at the top of the stairs, scratching his bum through his striped pyjamas. 'What kind of time do you call this?' he croaked.

'Breakfast time, sleepy head. What've you got?'

Flea grabbed my arm and gripped it tight, but his voice was calm. 'Don't forget it's today, Joseph.'

Rocky was plodding down the stairs. 'Oh, leave him alone, Flea. Just give him the morning off. He can help you save the planet this afternoon. He still owes me a left-handed race. Anyway, while we're playing, we have some important business to discuss.'

I looked at Flea, and shrugged my shoulders.

'We're going to be OK. I promise. Just relax, watch some cartoons or something, and I'll see you at midday at the latest.'

The Old Sycamore

It was one o'clock by the time I emerged from the Playstation pit. I wandered blinking outside into a hazy Mediterranean heat where I found my dad in the driveway cleaning the car. I paused.

'Nah, don't worry, Joseph,' he laughed. 'You're safe. Just thought I'd give the old girl a once over.' He looked fondly at his car. 'You were right, she is a bit on the grubby side. I'm taking her into town so I want her to look her best.'

His ancient brick of a phone rang. 'Hello? This is he.' He listened for a moment. 'Yes, that's great. I can be there by four thirty.'

He hung up. 'That's the opticians. They've done my specs, so I'll have 'em for tonight if I go to town a bit early. Is that OK?'

I nodded, realizing this meant I wouldn't have my dad around if I needed him when the person from

RIPS came. But most of our evidence was strong, and, if things got difficult I could always phone him on his mobile. I knew he'd come straight back if I needed him.

'Good on yer,' said my dad. 'I'll lock up when I leave, so you just get your overnight stuff this afternoon and I'll see you later.'

'OK.' I went to walk away, but he called me back.

'Oh, Joseph, just one more thing.' As I turned I felt Klaris shout, *Duck!* I threw myself behind the car and the sponge missed my head by an inch. I ran out and grabbed it—it was still half-full of water—and I lobbed it straight back at him.

My dad put up his arm to deflect the soggy missile, but he'd forgotten he was still holding the brick. He managed to avoid a sponge in the face but the force of it knocked the phone out of his hand and straight into the bucket of dirty, soapy water.

I didn't look back as I ran straight round to the Cliffs' to find Flea. He wasn't at home, but eventually I found him sitting down by the Island, dangling his feet in the water.

'Be careful,' I said. 'You really don't want to fall in there.'

He looked up, but he was struggling to hear me over the top of another voice. 'Is she worried?' I asked, and he nodded.

We sat quietly for a while. Klaris wasn't talking any more, but I could feel her nearby, like a heartbeat.

'I think we've ticked most of the stuff off the list,' I said, breaking the silence. 'There's one left, number seven, but I'll think of something. Like your dad said, they're highly skilled professionals and they won't carry out any medical procedure unless it's absolutely necessary.'

'She thinks we should run away,' said Flea, staring straight ahead. 'Over to the Island. She wants you to climb up the old burnt sycamore. I've told her that we can't hide for ever and we're going to stand and fight, but she's worried. She says they won't play fair.'

'Huh, shows what she knows,' I said. 'Well, you can relax, Flea. Because this is going to be a piece of cake.'

Dyed-Black Sideburns

At least he wasn't wearing the silver jumpsuit.

Mr Jones, Tyler and Ethan's dad, slicked down his black quiff and rang the doorbell at exactly four o'clock.

I saw him arrive and thought he must've come round to complain about the dog fight, but when Dr Cliff let him in then called us into the living room my heart sank. He was wearing a badge, pinned onto his denim cowboy shirt, that said, 'V. Jones, RIPS Co-ordinator.'

The last time I'd seen Mr Jones he was singing *Love Me Tender* at the village fete with his Elvis tribute band. But since then he'd put his music career on hold and retrained, as he explained to Dr Cliff.

'Life on the road is no good for the family, specially for the kids. My Ethan and Tyler, they're such sensitive little boys, and they miss their daddy. So when I heard about this job, I thought it sounded perfect. I had to do a week-long course, you know,' he told us. 'Lots of stuff to learn. Cos you've gotta be properly qualified to catch these little buggers, scuse my French. Course,' he leaned back in the sofa and wiped the trickle of sweat that was running down the side of his face into his dyed-black sideburns, 'I used to run a pest control business, and it's not really a lot different to that—except you don't get to kill 'em yourself. The hospital does that bit.'

He flashed us a whitened grin. 'So, you're the young 'uns with the little problem, are you?'

Flea stared at him, I managed a nod.

'Good, well I'm your man. Let's just take some details, and then we can pop you both in the van and get you up to the hospital for the . . . er, for your treatment.' He pulled some forms from his bag and scribbled on the back of one of them with an old biro until it started working.

'Right, let's start with full names.'

'Felix Peregrine Cliff,' said Flea's dad. 'But surely you won't be taking them to the hospital today? I thought this would be purely a diagnostic session.'

Mr Jones handed the forms over. 'Nope. I need to get them to the hospital this afternoon. Think you'd better do the little chap's spelling. Don't want to get that wrong.' He turned to me. 'What's your full name, young man? Not something hard, I hope.'

'Joseph Reece,' I said. 'But you can't take us for the Cosh. You haven't got permission from my dad.'

'Don't need it,' said Mr Jones, starting to look irritated. 'You two are classified as a Medical Emergency.'

'We can't be,' I said, my voice sounding wobbly. 'And anyway we have proof that Klaris isn't dangerous.'

He didn't look up from the form. 'Is that with one f?'

Dr Cliff cleared his voice, 'Joseph, let me deal with this. Now, look here, Mr Jones, I was definitely led to believe—'

He laid down his biro. 'New rules, Dr Cliff, under the Shorefield Charter. Cos of the amount of dangerous rogues around they're fast-tracking 'em. It's now down to a qualified technician, such as yours truly, to make all decisions about who does and who doesn't need treatment. I've looked at the file and I've decided. Now, unless there is overwhelming evidence to the contrary, I suggest we get on with transferring these two up to the hospital.'

'Yes, there is evidence! Loads of it!' I turned to Dr Cliff. 'We took your list, and we have proof that Klaris didn't do any of it. Well, most of it anyway.'

Dr Cliff's gaze swung from us to Mr Jones, and he went from looking angry to confused through to deflated, and then really, really tired.

For the first time Flea spoke. 'We thought it was someone trying to frame her, but it—oh, please can we just show you then you'll understand?'

Mr Jones was squinting at his watch. 'Well, only if it doesn't take too long. I have to get you two delivered to the hospital by five. An' I won't get paid unless I do.'

Number One

Flea walked to the door, 'Come on then, we've got a lot to see. First stop is my dad's car.'

With Flea in the lead we all headed out to the driveway and lined up on the gravel next to Dr Cliff's grey family saloon.

'Number one on Dad's list,' said Flea, 'is the turning on and not turning off again of the car lights.'

Mr Jones was nodding. 'Ah, yes, typical imaginary person mischief.'

'Dr Cliff,' I said, 'Do you smoke?'

'What? No, of course not, I'm a doctor. Filthy habit.'

'Flea, open the car door,' I said. As the battery was flat, Flea had to put the key in the lock and turn it.

We all peered in.

'And?' asked Dr Cliff.

'Open the ashtray.'

Flea climbed into the driver's seat and flipped it open. It was stuffed with cigarette ends.

'You boys been smokin'?' asked Mr Jones.

'No, not us—Mrs Cliff, Flea's mum,' I explained. 'Everyone nags her about smoking, so she does it in secret; hanging out of windows, in the garden, and sometimes she sits in the car to have a cigarette at night. She told me she turns on the little interior light. And sometimes she forgets to turn it off when she's finished, so the battery goes flat.'

Mr Jones was nodding. 'I see. Makes sense. OK. One nil to you two then. I'll cross that off the list.'

Number Two

'Follow me for number two!' Flea handed the keys to his dad and led the way back into the house and upstairs.

He stopped outside Dr Cliff's study and waited for us to catch up, then we all filed into the gloom. The heavy curtains were drawn only a few inches and dust motes danced in a thin stripe of sunlight. Dr Cliff's oak desk was piled high with files, and dirty coffee cups were positioned in the gaps between them. I looked for the wedding photograph I'd seen the day before but it had disappeared. I still needed something to help me explain the last accusation. But there was no clue, or none that I could see there, and Flea was starting to talk.

'Number two: the mystery of the shrinking stethoscope.'

There was a knock at the door and Pooh stepped in, looking sulky.

'Mr Jones, this is my sister Pooh, er, Prudence Cliff.'

'Is this going to take long, Flea?' she said. 'I do have other things to do.' She then coughed, a long, hard, painful-sounding cough.

'Thanks, Pooh, that's all we needed.'

'That's a nasty cough,' said Mr Jones as Pooh left the room. 'Lucky you've got a doctor in the house, eh? So, what did you diagnose, Dr Cliff?'

'Er,' Dr Cliff rubbed the back of his neck, 'I didn't need to diagnose anything because it's just a simple upper respiratory tract infection caused by a seasonal virus.'

'What, so you didn't listen to her chest?' Mr Jones looked surprised. 'I thought doctors always did that.'

'No, not this time,' he snapped.

'That's the problem,' said Flea. 'Dad wouldn't take her cough seriously, and Pooh doesn't like being ignored, so she decided to play a little trick on him.'

I picked up the stunted stethoscope from the desk.

'Dr Cliff assumed that Klaris had tampered with this,' I said. 'But actually, the answer was a lot simpler. Pooh did it, Dr Cliff. She's given me the glue she used to stick it with as evidence.' I held up the little pot.

'Nice one kids,' said Mr Jones. 'Well, looks like it's two nil to the young 'uns.' He checked his watch. 'Now, time's getting short, so if we could hurry this up a bit?'

'Yes, we'll be quick,' said Flea. 'Follow me, everyone.'

Number Three

We all traipsed back outside and Flea led us to the old rabbit hutch that was still in its place near the shed.

'Number three, the murder of Barry White the rabbit,' I announced. 'Call the witnesses, Flea.'

Flea whistled and the dogs came ambling round to us, Henry wagging contentedly, and Annie looking tired in the heat.

'Dr Cliff believes that, under pressure from Klaris, the dogs killed Barry,' I said.

Mr Jones nodded, 'Incidences of this type are commoner than you'd like to think. Under the influence of a rogue even man's best friend can turn into a savage beast.'

'Dr Cliff,' I said. 'Annie and Henry are your dogs, aren't they?'

Flea's dad nodded. 'Well, they're family pets really, but they definitely see me as their pack leader.'

'And they'd do anything you say?'

'Well, the Labrador is by nature a compliant dog. So, yes, I would say so.'

At that moment Rocky appeared. He was carrying a small square cage. He put it on the ground and took a sleepy golden hamster out from its fluffy bed and handed it to me. 'Your humble servant at your command, Master.' He bowed to me.

'Thanks, Rocky.'

'I've gotta have him back in half an hour, before Greg's sister gets home from swimming,' he said. 'So hurry up.'

'Good luck,' I whispered to the hamster, and placed him on the straw near the back of the hutch and shut the door.

'Now, Dr Cliff, we'd like you to order the dogs to eat the hamster.'

Dr Cliff looked shocked. 'No, I couldn't do that.'

Flea put his hand on his dad's arm. 'Go on, Dad, please. Do it for me. It'll be OK, I promise.'

He hesitated.

'If it looks like the hamster's in any danger you can call them off straightaway,' I said.

Dr Cliff still looked unconvinced, but he sighed, 'Oh, all right then.'

I opened the door and Dr Cliff reluctantly encouraged Annie and Henry to stick their heads in. 'Go on, dogs, find it.'

Annie and Henry didn't need telling twice. They went up on their hind legs and sniffed inside the hutch greedily, with Henry the first to find the hamster, which had curled up in the straw and gone back to sleep. I held my breath.

Henry was still sniffing the hamster all over when Annie joined in, their tails wagging in perfect synchronicity, and then they both started licking it.

'Tell them again,' I said to Dr Cliff.

'Go on Henry, go on Annie,' he said sadly, 'kill the hamster.'

Henry's yelp cut through his master's words, as he jerked his head back suddenly and turned back to Dr Cliff, with Annie close behind.

We could see a small bead of blood forming on Henry's black nose.

'Looks like that was one nil to the hamster,' laughed Mr Jones. 'My Digger would've had that in one mouthful. Not exactly the aggressive type, are they?'

'Labradors aren't bred for aggression,' said Dr Cliff stiffly.

'See,' I said, 'The dogs love you. If they won't kill something because you told them to, I don't think they'd do it for Klaris, do you?'

Flea returned the hamster to its cage.

'So, the death of the rabbit remains a mystery then,' said Mr Jones.

'No, actually we think we know who did it.' I said,

holding out the blurry photo I'd taken from under the apple tree earlier in the week.

'*Vulpes vulpes*,' said Flea. 'The indigenous British fox. This one was seen scavenging around the back garden just a few days ago. It comes right up to the house to raid our bins. We think that one night it spotted poor Barry White through the open French windows and took its chance.' He shook his head. 'It's what wild animals have to do to survive.'

'So,' said Mr Jones, 'Three nil. You really have done your homework, kids, I'll give you that. But I am running out of time, so if we could just get on.'

Number Four

Flea was already leading us into the living room, where he took down a book from the shelf: *Wood's Guide to Dog Breeding*.

'Number four—the drunken dogs.'

'The person responsible for this—' I began, but then Rocky came into the room, minus the hamster.

'It was me, Dad.'

Dr Cliff's face flushed a deep purple. 'You? You gave the dogs whisky? You stupid, stupid boy! Surely you know what alcohol can do?'

'Just let him explain,' I said. 'Please.'

So Rocky told his dad all about putting the drink in their bowls so they would get frisky.

'But I still don't understand why you would do that,' his dad said. 'Were you so desperate to have puppies?'

Rocky shrugged. 'No, I don't particularly like dogs.'

'Then why?'

Rocky looked at me, Flea and Mr Jones, and I thought for a moment that it was too painful and embarrassing for him to talk about it in front of other people. But then he answered, 'Because, Dad, the dogs are the only thing you care about, and I wanted to make you happy for a change.' He turned and walked out of the room leaving Dr Cliff's mouth gaping.

Flea turned to Mr Jones. 'Four nil,' he said, smiling. 'This way, everybody.'

So, with Dr Cliff close to tears, we walked outside, and followed Flea into the garden and round to the back of the shed.

Number Five

'Number five,' Flea announced. 'The carving of Klaris's name on the shed.'

'Now, this is something that definitely fits the profile of the classic rogue,' said Mr Jones. 'They love leaving their mark.'

'Wrong again,' said Flea. 'It was the twins—my brothers William and Edgar. Me and Joseph were out in the garden on Monday evening and we saw them disappear behind the shed for about ten minutes.'

'That doesn't prove anything,' said Mr Jones. 'It could just be a coincidence.'

'Yes,' I said. 'That's why I got this—a signed confession from Wills. But first I asked him to write Klaris's name. Look,' I pointed to the bottom of the sheet.

CLARIS

'He's spelt it wrong,' I said.

'And we know that Klaris would never do that,' Flea added.

'Well, we'll have to take your word for that, young man,' said Mr Jones. But, yes, I'd say you've done it again. So it's . . .'

'Five.'

'Yes, five nil to you.'

Flea grinned, and I allowed myself a small smile. It was going so well that if I hadn't had to worry about number seven I would've been feeling ecstatic.

'Come on, everyone,' said Flea. 'Not far for this one.'

Number Six

Flea led us to a flowerbed on the other side of the garden.

'Number six—migration,' I said. 'One of the reasons Dr Cliff called in RIPS was because he found out that Klaris was communicating with me.' I looked at Flea who gave me a little encouraging smile. 'I'm not going to deny this.'

Mr Jones shook his head. 'So, at last one point for the adults?'

'No, sorry. Because the truth is that I'm not the only one. You see, over the last few years Klaris has communicated with . . . well, I promised I wouldn't give any names, but another one of the Cliff kids. Anyway, Klaris was around for a while, then she went again, and she never became dangerous or even particularly annoying. According to this other family member they just used to play together. Obviously I can't show you any photos of this, but I may have some proof. They used to dig in the flowerbeds looking for interesting stuff. They would re-bury their 'treasure', as they called it, in little boxes they decorated.'

Flea had disappeared for a moment, but was back holding a shovel.

'Hopefully, we can prove that this is what they got up to, and you'll see that Klaris "migrating" is no more than making friends with a couple of other people, not a sign that she's turning rogue.'

I handed the shovel to Mr Jones.

'Can you dig here? It shouldn't be very deep.'

So Mr Jones positioned the blade where I showed him and dug into the hard earth. He had to break through roots and move stones, but about six inches down he came across a half decomposed cardboard box. The lid was caved in, and grey with dirt, but you could just about make out the felt tip patterns and the words, 'Our treasure. Belongs to me and Klaris. So keep out.'

'Go on,' I said. 'Open it.'

So he did. And inside was a perfect white heart-shaped stone.

Mr Jones nodded. 'Very good, boys. That's six nil to you. But if you've finished we're really going to have to get on with this. I've still got a bit of paperwork to fill in. So perhaps we could go back inside while I do that?'

Number Seven

We went into the house, this time me and Flea following Mr Jones and Dr Cliff. I was fizzing with joy. I knew we'd done it. Mr Jones had been all smiles and the one complaint left was unlikely to be a problem. He couldn't have us coshed just because Dr and Mrs Cliff were going through a bad patch.

Anyway it seemed that Flea was not going to leave it to chance. Once we were back in the living room, where Mr Jones was sorting through his forms, Flea said, 'We still have to do number seven—marital problems.'

'Eh?' said Mr Jones.

'It's the last one on the list.'

He checked his paperwork. 'Oh, yes, you're right. Go on then, we may as well get to the end.'

I took a deep breath, unsure of what I was going to say. But before I had made a sound, Flea began talking.

'This one's hard to explain, Dad, cos we're kids and we don't know about stuff like that. Anyway, we realize you're worried about Mum getting fed up and leaving you. So I phoned her at the hospital today and I asked her what makes a perfect husband, and she said she would settle for someone who wasn't grumpy all the time and would sit and have a chat with her once in a while instead of watching the news. She also said she'd like to go out together sometimes for a meal. And there was something else, erm . . . I know, she said a perfect husband brings their wife a cup of tea in bed. And, apparently, you haven't bought her tea in bed since 1998. So, you see, Dad, Klaris isn't trying to ruin your marriage. It's you.'

Mr Jones was nodding. 'Wise words from the young one. What marriage needs is effort. Let me think what Elvis, the King, would say on the subject,' and he stood up, feet astride, shut his eyes for moment, then curled his top lip, took a deep breath, opened his eyes again and sang:

Here's one for your honey
You gotta know
Love's always ready
To grow and grow

But don't ya
Sit back and watch the news

Don't do anything
And it's you who's gonna lose

Well, you could bring her tea
On a tray
A nice meal out
Would make her day

Do everything that she asks of you
Cos u-huh Doctor
She's feelin' blue

So don't ya
Sit back and watch the news
Don't do anything
And it's you who's gonna lose

Cos she cleans your house
And your car
Makes you jam
In an old fruit jar

So do everything that she asks of you
Cos u-huh Doctor
She's feelin' blue

So don't you
Sit back and watch the news
If you don't do anything
It's she who's a-gonna choose

Rocky and Pooh had come in to hear the singing. He really did sound like Elvis Presley, and, when Mr Jones had finished, we all clapped, he bowed, and said, 'Thangyaverymudge.'

Flea hugged his dad, then hugged me and said, with tears in his eyes, 'We did it!'

Mr Jones smoothed his quiff back again, then started going through his bag. 'Yes, you did very well, boys,' he said.

'So, we can go?' asked Flea, beaming so wide I thought his face would split.

'Sorry, but no,' replied Mr Jones, pulling out a heavy file. 'There's all this as well, you see.'

Zap and It's Gone

He handed me the file. It was an inch thick and made up of emails, typed letters, handwritten letters, and scribbled notes, with important parts highlighted in pink.

'That Klaris IS a THIEF'

'At first I thought it was a technical fault, but then I realized that the problems with my computer started when Klaris moved in with the Cliff family just down the road. I've spoken to my Internet Service Provider and they have confirmed that their equipment is working perfectly . . . '

'I never had headaches until I met the Cliff boy in the High Street. He looked at me strangely, and to this day, I've had a throbbing pain in my temples. The doctors have washed their hands of me, they say...'

'IF YOU DON'T DO SOMETHING ABOUT KLARIS CLIFF, WE WILL.'

My hands were shaking as I put the file down. Flea was rocking very slightly, and I could feel Klaris talking to him.

'You see,' explained Mr Jones, 'with all these complaints the Council can't just ignore it. Cos what if something tragic was to 'appen? Hmm? What would people say then? Well, I'll tell you, they'd blame us.'

Dr Cliff's face had gone a greyish-yellow colour, like

a fading bruise, and he looked as helpless as we felt.

Mr Jones turned to him. 'Course, as the father, they'd blame you even more.'

'So why the hell did you let the boys go through all that?' snapped Dr Cliff, his jowls vibrating in anger.

'Oh, it's the rules. We have to give all evidence a proper hearing. Wouldn't be fair otherwise.' He rubbed his hands together and smiled. 'Right then, let's get on. Now, you're a medical man, Dr Cliff, so I don't need to tell you that the procedure is nothin' to worry about. It's just like lancing a boil. Less serious even, cos there's no pus and blood. Just one zap and it's gone.'

But I wasn't listening. Whatever proof we'd found it would never have been enough, because the whole village was against us.

Mr Jones took out some more forms and started completing them slowly. My stomach felt like it had turned itself inside out and the adrenaline shooting down my arms and legs was making it impossible to sit still, so I stood up, and, as I did, I noticed a movement through the window.

It was Rocky out on the driveway, leaping up and down and grinning like an idiot. He was holding something up in one hand. It looked like a piece of wire, and he was giving a 'thumbs up' sign with the other.

'It's harmless really, Dr Cliff. They just find the right

area and they reduce it to prevent any more problems. So there's nothing to worry about. Nothing at all. I'll get them home in a couple of hours with just a slight headache, and no more imagination between them than a potato.'

He turned to us. 'How does that sound, boys?'

'Can't wait,' I said. 'Can I go first?'

Mr Jones chuckled, 'I'm afraid the hospital will have to decide that. But, if you like, I can put in a good word for you.'

Dr Cliff cleared his throat. 'Now, surely we can—' But Mr Jones had grabbed me and Flea and was pulling us out to the driveway.

Flea's face was frozen in fear. I took his hand and squeezed it but I couldn't tell him what Rocky had done because I didn't know myself. I was relying on his talent for breaking things though, so I felt pretty confident.

'Now, look here, before you take them anywhere—' Dr Cliff tried again, but it was obvious that, as far as Mr Jones was concerned, the time for talking was over.

The Elvismobile was parked next to Dr Cliff's saloon. It was silver, and had a picture of Mr Jones on the side dressed in a white spangly suit with a huge seventies collar. He opened the double doors at the back.

'Hop aboard the tour bus, boys. Sit anywhere you like.' We peered in, but there were no seats. Mr Jones saw the shock on Dr Cliff's face. 'It's not far. My boys love bouncing around in the back. It's done them no harm at all.'

'No, no, no,' said Dr Cliff. 'I don't think I can allow this.'

But Mr Jones pushed us in and slammed the doors shut.

From inside I heard Flea's dad finally lose his temper. 'Open those doors at once, damn you! I've got friends in high places at the hospital, and I forbid you to take these children away until I've spoken to your superior.'

'You *forbid* me?' Mr Jones snorted. 'She's a pest, and, in my professional opinion, these kids need their brains frying.' He opened the driver's side door. 'And if I don't get them in to be done, I don't get paid, so move out of the way old man and let me get on with my job.'

The van rocked as he got in and slammed the door behind him. This was followed by the sound of Dr Cliff hammering on the side and yelling, 'Open up! I demand that you let those boys out!'

Flea huddled up next to me on the wheel arch and I held my breath as Mr Jones put his keys in the ignition and turned. There was a click, and then silence.

'What the—' he said, and tried again. Nothing.

He climbed out. 'Dr Cliff, we seem to be having a little difficulty. You wouldn't mind giving me a jump start?'

Flea's dad laughed. 'You've seen the demonstration. I'm afraid that, as usual, my car has a flat battery.'

Mr Jones muttered something rude about phone signals and people living in the middle of bloody nowhere as he came round to the back.

'These two can come out while I use your phone to call the garage, but only cos it's so hot they'd cook if I left them in there.'

He turned to us, and his voice was threatening. 'But don't even think of runnin' away. Yer still booked in.'

'Don't worry,' I said. 'We wouldn't miss it for the world.'

A Distant Woof

Dr Cliff sat at the kitchen table with us, his face buried in his hands. 'I didn't know. I thought . . . I thought it would be a chat, some preliminary diagnostic tests perhaps. I had no idea about the other letters. I'd noticed people acting strangely towards me, and I've been losing patients for months, but I couldn't work out why.' He blew his nose. 'I can't believe it. They've blamed her for everything that's gone wrong in the village.'

He looked at me, his saggy eyes full of tears. 'I need to go and see your dad, Joseph. I should never have contacted the Council without telling him. It's unforgivable of me. I'll go and see him now. If I explain everything he'll understand. You wait here.'

I let him go, though I knew that by now my dad would be out, and, with the soapy swim that his phone had taken earlier, there would be no way of contacting him.

Rocky whistled long and low.

'Near miss, Joseph, my old mate. Good thing I watch Thief School, or you'd be under the fryer right now.'

'Yeah, thanks for that. But how did Thief School help?'

'Well, I was trying to hot-wire his van and drive it off. But a bit broke off in my hands.'

'So, what are you two going to do now?' asked Pooh. 'He'll sort out some transport soon.'

'I dunno.' I said. 'Wait for a miracle? Run away?'

'Looks like someone's already had that idea,' said Rocky, nodding at the empty chair where Flea had been sitting.

'He's probably just in the loo,' said Pooh. 'He'll be back in a moment.'

'Nah,' said Rocky. 'Not unless he's taken to doing it in the fresh air. I saw him go past that window about two minutes ago. He's definitely done a runner.'

'The dogs have gone too,' noticed Pooh.

'He's really scared.' I said. 'I think we should go and find him.'

'OK,' said Pooh. 'I'll stay here with Egg in case he comes back. You two go and have a look round.'

We checked the house and garden, then ran into the field and followed the footpath down towards the Island. The weather was getting unbearable, and the air was dotted with thunder flies that flew in our mouths and up our noses.

'It's so hot the dogs have probably gone in the river,' said Rocky, spitting out the little black specks.

'Really?'

'Yeah, they love a swim when it's boiling. But my dad hates them going in there cos the water's so weedy. He says it's lethal and they could easily get dragged under.'

Despite the heat I felt myself turn cold. I used to think that was just something they write in books, but it really happened.

'You don't think Flea would go in after them, do you? I mean if someone he really trusted told him to?'

Rocky laughed. 'Flea? Mr Health and Safety who wears his armbands in the shallow end of the swimming pool? No, course not.' But we sprinted the rest of the way to the river anyway. When we got there the only sign of Flea or the dogs was a big pile of yellow diarrhoea.

'So we know where they've been,' said Rocky. 'I'd recognize one of Annie's sloppy poos anywhere. Let's head home, he's bound to be there by now.'

Back at the house we ran into the kitchen, expecting to see Flea, but it was still just Egg and Pooh sitting at the table.

'Haven't you found him yet?'

I explained about the calling card left by Annie.

She frowned. 'Was your dad's boat still there?'

'We didn't look, but it must be. It's locked up and the only key is inside Wills at the hospital.'

Pooh started pacing around the kitchen using her dad's list as a fan to keep herself cool. Egg and Rocky slumped over on the table, exhausted by the heat.

Then, as we waited for someone to take control, we heard a boom in the distance. We looked at each other. Pooh voiced what we were all thinking.

'Oh, God. Someone's shooting on the Island. What if Flea and the dogs are there and the hunters don't spot them?' She was heading for the door. 'Come on.'

'Wait,' I said. 'Just tell your dad. He'll know what to do.'

She shook her head. 'He's taken Rocky's bike and gone up to the hospital. He's mates with someone senior up there. He's going to try and get them to delay the Cosh till they've had a chance for proper tests.'

'And what about Mr Jones?'

'The garage said they can't come until Monday. He didn't look too happy when he realized you and Flea had disappeared, and he ran off looking for you. I think we'd better find Flea before he does.'

She grabbed Egg by the arm, and he started whining, 'I've got a tummy ache. I need to go to the toilet.'

But Pooh pulled him roughly through the door. 'You can go later, Egg. We've got to find Flea first.'

He started to cry. 'Stop! You're hurting me!'

Rocky stepped in. 'Let go of him. I'll stay here while he goes to the loo, and we'll catch you two up.'

Pooh dropped Egg's arm and ran out with me trailing behind. I stopped as we passed my back door and tried the handle, hoping that my dad had decided not to go out after all. I was finally ready to tell him everything and let him fix it all for me. But my dad was out and the door was locked.

There was no other option, so I caught up with Pooh and we sprinted together up to the Island. All the way along the rough path the gunshots got louder and more frequent. But by the time we could see the Island we'd both heard something else too—something worse—barking.

Pooh started shouting, 'Flea! Henry! Annie!' But the only reply was a distant woof.

I turned to Pooh, 'That could be a hunter's dog.'

She shook her head. 'Dad doesn't let them take dogs over cos they disturb the nesting birds. It's definitely Henry's bark, so Flea is either over there with the dogs, or . . .' Pooh paused and looked down into the dark green river.

She started to move along the bank. 'We've got to get over there before anyone gets hurt.'

'We can't. The boat's locked up.'

'So?'

'So there's no other way over, unless you want to swim and risk drowning yourself just to add to the body count.'

'Well, I'm not going to sit here while Flea's in

danger, Joseph. It's not far. You can do what you want, but I'm going in.'

'Wait! Just let me just see if I can do something with the chain.'

I scrambled down to the little wooden boat and tugged at the heavy chain, hoping the padlock might fly open.

'How does it look?' she called down.

'Solid,' I said. 'You got a hairpin or something so I can try and pick the lock?'

Pooh's eyes flashed with annoyance. 'A hairpin? Perhaps you'd like a piece of whale bone from my corset as well? What century do you think this is? And since when did you know how to pick locks anyway?'

'Well, I don't really. But it always looks easy on the telly.'

Pooh bit her lip, which I guessed was to stop herself from shouting at me. When she spoke it was slowly and clearly. 'We can't waste any more time. My little brother could be shot at any moment, so I'm going to swim over this river. Are you coming or not?'

I looked across the water. A large area of its smooth dark surface was broken by weeds, like the tip of an iceberg, and I shook my head. 'No, neither of us should risk it.'

She groaned and started taking off her shoes.

'Wait,' I said. 'I've got an idea. See that ring that the

chain goes through? It's just held onto the boat by a couple of rusty screws. I reckon I could kick it off.'

She paused. 'OK, I'll give you one minute,' she said. 'Then I'm swimming across.'

I pulled the boat right up to the bank, handed the chain to Pooh, and said, 'Hold this, but be prepared to step back when it breaks.'

Taking a deep breath and, using the power of my whole body behind my leg I kicked with the force and precision of a premiership footballer taking a penalty in the World Cup. As my leg flew up an imaginary crowd roared in my head, and my trainer, which I hadn't bothered lacing, took flight like a baby bird arcing away to freedom in the direction of the river. And then, what felt like seconds later, I finally hit my target, with my foot smashing into the surprisingly hard metal ring, and I heard a crunch.

Unfortunately the crunch came from my toe. The hook was still firmly attached to the boat.

The scenario playing in my head vanished immediately and was replaced by a pain that made every time I'd ever stubbed my toe seem like a tickle in comparison. I fell over and rolled in agony for a bit, then I pulled my sock off and I gasped when I saw my big toe. It was branching away from the others, the skin was turning a stormy purple and blood was pooling under the nail.

'Oh, God,' said Pooh. 'What have you done now?'

'I think I heard it break,' I gasped.

'Well, that settles it. You wait here for the others. I'm going in.'

I started to argue, but she wouldn't listen. 'We don't have any alternatives. Anyway, even when you're not injured I'm a better swimmer than you.'

My male pride surged, and I was about to argue with her when my toe gave an almighty twinge and I threw up right by her feet.

Pooh took a step back, 'Oh, great. Now I've got puke on my shoes.'

She had begun to empty her pockets, getting ready to step into the water, when we heard the sound of running coming closer. A second later Rocky and Egg came around the corner, and they were smiling.

Deep Green Web

Pooh went to meet them. 'Have you found him?' she asked.

Rocky shook his head, then noticed me. 'What're you lying around for, Joseph?'

I pointed to my toe.

'Ugh, that's horrible, put it away.'

'So, why are you looking so pleased with yourself?' Pooh asked him.

'Well, Flea hasn't turned up yet, but *this* has.'

Rocky held out a sandwich bag with a small key inside. It was the padlock key.

I was confused. 'But where did you get a spare key?'

He grinned. 'It's not a spare. It's *the* key.'

'Wills is back? Talk about good timing.'

'Nope. Have another guess.' Rocky grinned.

Pooh was getting impatient. 'Just give it to me, for God's sake.' She grabbed the little bag. 'Why's it in here?' She opened the bag and then closed it again quickly. 'Hey, this stinks!'

Rocky and Egg laughed. 'I did wipe it with some tissue,' said Rocky. 'You should've smelled it when it was freshly laid.'

'I still don't understand,' I said. 'Where did you get it?'

'You know I stayed back with Egg while he went to the toilet?' I nodded. 'Well, I was just hanging round outside the door and I heard it hit the pan. It kind of clanked and I guessed right away what had happened.'

I turned to Egg. 'So it was *you* after all! *You* swallowed the key. Why did you let Wills take the blame?'

His dark owl eyes blinked slowly in response. I should have guessed. Egg and Wills thought of themselves as one person, so it wasn't important which one had actually swallowed the key. *They* had swallowed it and that was all that mattered.

'I can't believe I'm doing this,' said Pooh, holding the end of the key by the plastic bag and inserting it into the padlock. The lock clicked open and the chain slithered to the ground.

I couldn't do much more than hobble, but Rocky helped me up and into the boat, and Pooh and Egg followed. It was a squeeze, and, with the weight of all four of us the rim of the hull was just inches from the murky water.

Pooh positioned herself in the middle, grabbed the oars from Rocky, and began to row across the river.

I wished that I could've been the one to take charge, but I had to admit that Pooh was pretty good, for a girl. As the blades ploughed through the water, I could see the muscles in her bare arms bunching into quite impressive mounds. I realized that she was probably stronger than me, and vowed to buy some weights if we got home alive.

Although the dank water was still lapping greedily at the boat, we were going pretty fast in the right direction when, half way across the stretch, one of the oars suddenly caught in the weeds and jerked right out of Pooh's hand.

As she fished it out Rocky grabbed my arm and whispered, 'Listen.'

'What?' I said. 'I can't hear anything.'

'Exactly,' he replied. The gunshots had stopped and so had the barking.

'Hurry up, Pooh,' I said. 'We have to get over there fast.' It was true, but really I was saying it to try and convince myself that Flea was on the Island and not below us, tangled inside the deep green web.

After two more stops to retrieve stuck oars Pooh got us across the weediest part of the river, and, just when I was ready to scream from the pain in my toe and the dread in my chest, we felt the underside of the boat scrape unhealthily on the bottom.

We had reached Goat Island.

Rocky and Pooh helped me clamber out of the boat, but we had a problem. With no sound coming from the dogs or the guns we didn't know where to head to, and where to avoid.

I was relieved when Pooh took charge again. 'Let's stick to the edge,' she said, and we started to walk in a clockwise direction around the shore of the Island.

'Flea! Henry! Annie!' we shouted as we went, with Egg's funny little high-pitched voice adding half a second behind, 'Where are you?' or 'We're here,' and once, 'Coming, ready or not.'

Our progress was seriously slow. It shouldn't have taken us more than ten minutes to get round the whole Island, but I could hardly walk. Rocky had offered me his shoulder, and I leant on him as a crutch, but I'm taller and heavier than him, and we must have looked like we were in a drunk three-legged race. I put my bare foot on the ground as little as possible, but whenever I did it always seemed to land on a sharp stone, or a thorny stick, or a piece of old barbed wire, and it was soon burning with stings and rips.

After half an hour the others were suffering too. Though it was late the weather was unbearably humid and the thunder flies were multiplying fast. But that was the least of our problems. The weeds and brambles tore at any exposed skin, and it was obviously a bumper year for stinging nettles too, so we were soon covered in black dots, sore white bumpy rashes, and broken pink and red trails like 'cut-here' marks. But we couldn't stop. We had to keep moving and calling for Flea until we found . . . well, that was something I tried not to think about.

It was when we were more than half way round the Island that the guns started up again.

Pooh cocked her head to one side. 'I think we're heading straight for the hunters. We need to think. If Flea is here, and not at the bottom of the river, where's he likely to go?'

You know how when people can't make a decision they say they're torn? Well, now I understand what they mean. I felt as though the molecules in the two halves of my body were literally moving in different directions and I was going to rip in half. I wanted to lead everyone back to the safe part of the Island, but I'd remembered my conversation with Flea from earlier, and I was pretty sure I knew where he was hiding.

And that meant walking straight into the line of fire.

Right to the Top

'Come on,' I said, 'I think they're this way.'

Pooh was looking at me as if I was mad, but she followed anyway. Egg, still marching next to her, stared straight ahead, his face expressionless. 'Don't worry,' I heard Pooh say to him, 'It's just like playing an adventure game.' She paused. 'Only this time it's real.'

I didn't hear if he replied because at that moment shots broke the air right over our heads. There was rustling and snapping as the branches above us parted and a dead pigeon thumped onto the ground at our feet.

Egg looked like he was going to cry, but Pooh put her arm around him and said, 'D'you know what, when we get back home I'm going to make us all hot chocolate with extra squirty cream.'

Egg nodded, stepped over the bird, and said, 'If Flea is dead I think I'll miss him.'

So we stumbled on, ducking every time a shot rang out, and we were nearly back at our starting point when Rocky turned to me, looking scared. 'I don't know what your plan is, Joseph. But I really don't want to get shot. Well, not unless I'm in a proper war in, like, a desert somewhere, or a real jungle or—'

And then I stopped listening because I'd spotted something.

It wasn't much more than a dent in the undergrowth where some of the grasses and weeds were bent or squashed, but I knew straight away that it was what we needed because it led directly to the biggest tree on the Island; the one I was looking for, the one Klaris had told Flea to go to, the burnt up, half rotted, mangled old sycamore.

I was used seeing it from the other side of the river, but close up it was an even stranger sight. Running down the charred trunk was a deep gash, where the lightning had tried to split the tree in two. Black splintered fingers splayed out to the left, marking where a huge limb had been ripped out that night. But on the right the branches were untouched by fire, and dried out leaves and bunches of boomerang-shaped seeds, the tree's final fruit, were rattling in the growing breeze.

With my teeth clamped together I let go of Rocky and did a sort of hobbling dash, half falling, half running, focusing on the black shapes panting and wagging at the foot of the tree. I hardly even noticed the new stinging sensation in my buttocks because there was something else far more important to worry about; Flea wasn't with them.

'Flea!' I called, looking around desperately, 'Flea!'

So, he had drowned after all, I thought. He was trapped in the weeds under the river and we must have rowed straight over him.

'Where is he?' I yelled at the dogs in desperation. 'Tell me, you stupid mutts!' They looked my way for a moment, then tipped their muzzles up towards the top of the tree.

So I looked up too and there, in the crook of a high branch, camouflaged by a few dead hand-shaped leaves, was Flea.

His clothes were wet and his pale hair was dark and full of bits of vegetation. His face was smudged with dirt and his eyes were closed. But when we called out his name he woke up.

He looked confused for a moment, then his eyes widened in fear and he shouted, 'Have you brought him here? The man who wants to zap Klaris?'

'No, he's not here. It's just us. I promise. You can come down now,' I said.

'Not yet. Klaris says you have to come up here. You didn't listen to her, so she's got to show you instead.'

'I can't, Flea.' I called up. 'It's really dangerous here. We have to go home. Your dad's trying to sort it out. It'll be OK. Please come down.'

'No. You come up here.'

'Flea. I've hurt my toe and—' I felt the back of my trousers, and my hand came back wet with blood. My blood. 'Oh my God, I think I've been shot in the bum.'

Even from the ground I could see his jaw jut out. 'If you want me to come down you'll have to climb up and get me. Otherwise I'm staying here all night.'

'But I've already told you, I'm injured. I can't climb a tree in this state.'

'And I've told *you* I'm staying here until you do.'

The sky was darkening as the thunderclouds that had been gathering joined together, masking the sun, and I felt the wind rise and the temperature drop.

Then Flea, from his perch, pointed beyond us. 'I can see him!' he screamed. 'He's coming! Mr Jones is coming, and he's going to take us away and you'll never know unless you come up here now!'

I looked behind me, and stumbling through the woods, dripping, and with tendrils of weed in his collapsed quiff, was Mr Jones. And he didn't look happy.

So I started to haul myself up the dying tree. The first few bare branches weren't too bad, but I'd barely climbed a man's height before there was a gap and I had to stop.

'Flea, I can't get any higher. You'll have to come down now.'

'Keep climbing!' he ordered.

'No, it hurts like hell and I might fall.'

'She says you have to go on.'

But I knew that myself.

Keep climbing, she said. *Right to the top. I need to show you something.*

'Just do what she says and then it'll all be over,' Flea shouted.

'No, Flea. I'm exhausted. I'm in pain. I can't climb up that far. I just can't do it.'

Mr Jones was at the bottom of the tree now. He growled a warning at Rocky and Egg, then shoved Pooh out of the way and started climbing up after us.

'You bloody nuisances, get down here now, or I'll pull you down and break your bloody necks. I'm not gonna miss out on my day's wages cos you two think it's funny to play hide 'n' seek. You're booked in and I'm gonna get you there, dead or alive.'

'Right to the top, Joseph,' squealed Flea. 'She says you have to be able to see over all the bushes behind the tree.'

I knew that too. Her voice was as clear as a thought of my own.

'What's he talking about?' shouted Mr Jones. 'What are you hiding from me behind the bushes? Is it more of those *things*?'

Now the bone-dry branches were straining and the tree was groaning. I wiped the sweat off my hands and pulled myself higher. Mr Jones was climbing up fast, and I tensed my body, waiting for him to grab me, but instead he trod on my fingers as he climbed past.

'You can't hide anything from me,' he said. 'I'm gonna see exactly what you're up to.' And he disappeared into the branches above.

Flea was still shouting frantically. 'Hurry, Joseph! Hurry! Get higher so you can see!'

So with a final push that made my foot burn like fire and ripped at the skin on my hands I reached the top, and, just as I did, I heard Mr Jones shout from nearby, 'Jesus Christ! What the hell's that down there?'

The branches started to tremble and release their last helicopter seeds, which spiralled all around like spinning confetti. Mr Jones was shouting 'Earthquake! Earthquake! It's the aftershock!' and I realized that it wasn't just the old sycamore shaking, the ground was too. Then the tree seemed to groan and sigh, and something large flew downwards past me, and there was a crash. And, for a second, there was silence.

Like the world on pause.

Then in my head I heard Klaris:

Joseph, my Joseph.

It was clearer than ever, and there was something else. It was familiar.

And I thought:

Klaris?

Kla . . . ris

Clai . . . ris

Claire . . . Reece

Klaris

'Mum?'

When she replied her voice vibrated through every cell of my body.

Joseph. I'm sorry.

'Y-y-you?' My jaw was quivering, and my teeth were chattering, but I managed to say. 'It's really you?'

Forgive me, my love.

'It can't be.'

Through the roar of my pain, exhaustion, and fear, I heard her say,

Joseph, I didn't mean to leave you. There was an accident.

My breath was coming faster and faster, and sweat, as cold as the river water, started running down my face.

'Mum, I . . .'

Then I felt something new inside me. It began to swell and grow solid and heavy like a lead balloon inflating, and it pressed so hard against my ribcage that I thought I was having a heart attack.

'It . . .'

I was trying to tell her it's OK, like I used to. To say, 'I understand', and 'I love you'. Only I didn't. Because when I managed to gain control of my mouth something else came out.

A howl.

And the sound, raw and grating, spewed on and on,

filling the Island with its ugliness and with all the hurt and disappointment she'd caused every time she'd let me down, every time she'd cried and I didn't know why, every time she'd made Dad sick with worry. But most of all I yelled all the loneliness and rage that I had felt every single minute of every single day since she went.

When I was empty, and the sound had drifted up into the full grey sky above us, she spoke again.

I wanted to surprise you. I came back on your birthday. I went home, made a picnic and brought it over here.

I was shaking my head. 'No, stop talking. You've told me enough.'

I tried to phone, but you weren't home. So I waited.

'I'm not ready to hear this.'

But I'd travelled overnight and I was tired.

'Stop it! Stop it! Stop it!'

I pressed my hands against my ears, but it just made her voice clearer, like when she used to come to say goodnight, and spoke softly as she kissed my cheek.

I fell asleep here.

'Shut up! Shut up!' I was desperate to get away from the sound, from the truth, 'Stop talking! I don't want to hear it!'

Then the storm started.

I was thrashing around, punching the air, kicking my legs and shaking my head like my brain was full of ants.

The leaves sheltered me from the rain.

'I said shut up! Why don't you listen? It was your choice to go away, Mum. You decided that you'd swan off to Spain and leave us, and now you drag me over to the Island and up this horrible old tree to tell me you're dead. You haven't been here for more than *two years*! Did you know that? I've been waiting for over two years! And you were here all the time but you decided not to tell me until now.' I dropped my voice to a spent whisper. 'You didn't care about me. So, why the hell should I care what happened to you?'

Then I felt a warmth curl around me like the hug she gave me on Flea's sofa, and I collapsed back onto the branch, as weak as a baby.

Then the lightning hit the tree. I never woke up.

Above us the first few drops of rain started to fall from the sky.

It's time, Joseph, she said. *Be brave.*

And I looked down.

At first I just saw the edges. It used to be turquoise and pink checks, but the colours had been faded by the rain and bleached by three summers. It was still stretched out in a square, held down on the corners with rocks. To one side were the wicker basket and a bottle of lemonade, the label washed blank. To the other was a pile of boxes, smothered with creepers, shreds of half-rotted wrapping paper poking through and flapping like flags.

A thick branch ripped from the sycamore tree lay

diagonally across the rug like a sash. And my mum's hippy sandals lay just next to the presents, neatly paired, like she'd only just put them there.

'Mum, was that you under there?'

Forgive me for leaving you, Joseph.

I whispered, 'I forgive you. And I won't ever tell you to go away again. Just say you'll stay with me here in my head.'

I can't.

'Please, don't go!' I said. 'Don't leave me. Not again.' But I knew from the stillness of the air that it was too late.

Then little coloured dots began to dance in front of my eyes, and they swirled and merged and I heard a high-pitched sound that blocked out the noise of Mr Jones screaming, and I couldn't remember to hold on any more, and everything went black.

The Last Traces

As I came to, lying in the bushes that had broken my fall, with everyone staring at me with big worried eyes, I wanted to laugh. It was so simple that I couldn't believe it had taken so long to work out.

But I didn't laugh, I cried instead because I remembered what it meant.

Klaris was my mum.

She was dead.

My mum was dead.

I tried to tell them what I had seen. I suppose they must've understood me through the sobs because there was a silence that seemed to suck the air out of the woods.

Then the sky finally cracked and the rain began to pelt down on us.

The hunters, their bags bulging with dead birds, found us soaked and shaking in the clearing under the tree.

As they towed the *Lady Claire* back behind their boat, Henry stood on the prow sniffing the chilled, stormy air.

I sat at the back with Flea, watching the Island move further away from us.

'I'm sorry,' he said. 'I didn't know.'

And he rubbed the last traces of the letter K from his forehead.

SATURDAY

Sunshine and Roses

When I woke up in hospital, groggy from painkillers, it took me a few moments to remember. Then everything came back to me like a horror movie in fast-forward.

Next to me was my dad, slumped in a chair snoring. I watched him for a while, then I leant over and pinched his nose to wake him up. When he opened his eyes they were pink and his lids were puffy, like he'd been punched.

'So . . .' he said, taking my hand and squeezing it hard. 'So, now we know what happened to your mum.' His eyes were shining with the tears he was holding back. 'I'm sorry you had to be the one to find out.'

I shrugged. 'Who told you?'

'The Cliff kids. After they got you in the ambulance they let themselves into the cottage with the spare key. I walked in and found them on the sofa drinking hot chocolate. Flea did most of the talking, but when he got upset they filled in for him.' My dad paused. 'Y'know, I never realized how close those kids are. Flea's lucky to have them. Especially now.'

He stood up and went to stare out of the window. His new clothes were creased and his hair was tangled at the back.

'I should've realized,' my dad said, turning round again. 'She would never have left you like that. We must've missed her call when we were in town picking up your birthday cake. That's when the rain started, d'you remember? We got soaked.' Then his words turned into gulps as the tears came pouring out.

'But why didn't we look for her, Dad?'

He blew his nose. 'Because . . . because I thought she didn't want to be found. Claire is,' he paused, 'Claire was a complicated person. She had these moods. It started after you were born. She had her good days, and everything was sunshine and roses, but the next day she'd withdraw into herself and I couldn't reach her. It was like she was locked in a cage. I learnt that I had to leave her alone and she'd always come back to us. I didn't know this time was different.' His voice went raspy and he had to stop before the tears took his words away again.

I felt like I should cry too, like everyone would expect me to. But I couldn't. I just felt empty. Empty and bruised on the inside.

We'd won. We'd escaped RIPS and the Cosh, but the

result was the same—Klaris was gone, and my mum was too, and, now that I knew she was dead, I would never ever imagine her coming back again.

What Happened Next

It was a year ago yesterday. But sometimes it feels like I've known Mum was dead for ever.

I'm lying back on the grass beside Pooh, and she's taking notes about what happened next for her book.

The coroner called her death a freak accident, a million to one tragedy, which Dad says Mum would have liked. She hated being normal.

'Do it in the proper order, Joseph,' says Pooh. 'Way before the inquest your file was closed.'

We had a phone call from RIPS saying that Mr Jones was no longer with the department, and our file had been found downstream, washed almost clean by the green water, and not legible enough to use. No evidence, no Cosh. So we were off the hook and off the list.

'Then they announced the Shorefield investigation.'

It was on the news that the Defence for Imaginary People had forced the government to launch an inquiry led by some world-famous expert who used to be on TV. But Dr Peasman says we shouldn't hold our breath because the dad of the family that died was linked to some important people, and it suits the government to blame an imaginary person. But meanwhile they've suspended all the RIPS departments, so no one else will get the Cosh, for a while anyway.

'Then it was Christmas.'

'You've forgotten autumn,' I say. 'The rainiest for fifty years. And then Christmas.' Not the best, but it happened, then it was over, and a new year began, as they do, even when your mum's dead and turned to ashes in a pot on the mantelpiece.

'It's not a pot, Joseph. It's called an urn.'

Whatever, Dad hated her being in there. He said that she should blow wild and free on the Island.

'So we built the bridge,' says Pooh. Dr Cliff was so appalled that Flea had swum the river that we clubbed together and had a rope bridge built that attaches to two big oaks and spans the river.

What was left of the old sycamore had to be cut down, but we made the stump into a seat, and scattered my mum's ashes around it.

'And Flea gave that speech,' says Pooh. Yes, and me and Dad cried as Flea told stories about how kind and clever she was, and left out all the bad bits. He'd lost his best friend that night, but Flea seemed to accept that it was time for her to go.

'He's really changed a lot, hasn't he?' I say to Pooh. Maybe he's just standing a bit straighter after everyone told him how brave (and stupid) he'd been. Or maybe he was just ready for a growth spurt, but by spring, when he turned eight, Flea towered over the twins and was catching Rocky up fast.

'We forgot the puppies,' says Pooh as we see three black Labradors come bounding out of the house. Annie's babies were born a few weeks afterwards. Flea stayed up all night with his dad helping with the births, and together they took care of the puppies until they went to their new homes.

Flea became an expert in dog breeding, and his dad said he could keep one.

'But,' Pooh reminds me, 'Mum said she'd leave if there was another dog to clean up after.'

So Flea persuaded his mum and dad to go to counselling to sort it out, and it must have gone well because Mrs Cliff and Glenfiddich the puppy are both still here. But now they call him Fido, because almost no one gets to keep their real name in that house.

Pooh's scribbling it all down as we talk because she wants to be a writer and has decided that her first book will be about Klaris.

'You're wasting your time,' I say, 'People are only interested in stuff that happens to celebrities.'

'You might not be famous,' she says, 'but to me you're a VIP.' And I feel myself blush.

Pooh looks up from her notes. 'D'you miss her?' she asks. 'I mean, d'you miss Klaris?'

'Sometimes,' I say. And I mean that whenever I'm ill, or lonely or upset, I'd do anything to have my mum back, even as Klaris inside my head.

'But not all the time, and definitely not right now,' I say to Pooh as I cross my fingers and lean towards her.

DAILY POST FRIDAY AUGUST 13

SHOREFIELD FAMILY FOUND DEAD in HOME

A British diplomat, his wife and two young children died yesterday in what police have described as a 'brutal attack.' Neighbours in the tree-lined street said the family, who had been living there for six months, were quiet and kept to themselves. The police have appealed for any information that might help with their enquiries.

DAILY POST SATURDAY AUGUST 14

DIPLOMAT DEATHS RIDDLE

Sources in Shorefield claim that an imaginary person has been named a suspect in the on-going murder enquiry. A police spokesperson stressed that investigations are still at an early stage. But, amid rising public fear of rogues, lawyers have warned that the case demonstrates the desperate need for tougher legislation on imaginary people.

DAILY POST MONDAY AUGUST 16

POLICE WARN ROGUE IMAGINARY PERSON at LARGE in SHOREFIELD

At a press conference today police confirmed rumours that an imaginary person, known only as Snow, is being sought for murder. Chief Inspector Dom

cont. p18

cont. from p2 Clifford said, 'While we urge the public not to panic, we would advise anyone who has recently gained an imaginary person to report immediately to their nearest police station or medical centre.'

DAILY POST WEDNESDAY AUGUST 18

PM SPEAKS OUT ON ROGUES

The Prime Minister, speaking today from the House of Commons, has defended the emergency powers given to RIPS practitioners in the wake of the Shorefield murders, saying, 'The COSH is perfectly safe and it is the only way to protect us all from the dangers of rogues.' But the Defence League for Imaginary People has issued a statement today accusing the government of a 'politically-motivated cover up.'

DAILY POST THURSDAY AUGUST 19

PARENTS QUEUE FOR COSH AMID FEARS OF KILLER ROGUES

Following the first showing last night of the government's 'If in doubt, zap it out!' campaign, there were scenes of panic across the country as parents demanded the new COSH treatment. Mother of four, Wanda Flynn, told us, 'We saw the ad and we're here because we're not willing to take any chances. I want all my kids done, and two of them haven't even got an imaginary person. But I'd rather be safe than sorry.'

Dear Reader

A strange thing led me to write this book; a recurring imaginary friend. She was a girl of about nine or ten whose name began with the letters Al, and she was imagined by my brother, myself, and, decades later, my own daughter.

In all three cases she was nice but bossy, a lot like a big sister. I also had twin imaginary-friend boys who were a bit younger than me, and I remember that she was quite mean to them. But never to me.

Was this just a coincidence, or was something else going on? When she was reincarnated the third time I was working as a journalist and I decided to write an article about imaginary friends. Among the many fascinating things I found in my research was the fact that in some places, including Japan, there are people who believe that imaginary friends are protective spirits who watch over children. Sometimes they are dead ancestors, and sometimes just body-less beings who found themselves needed.

I liked that idea, and from there grew Klaris, and a whole world where imaginary friends had substance, free will and people prepared to defend them.

In this book I also wanted to give a shout out to imagination, that weird substance as malleable as clay that seems to dry out as we grow up, and which we forget can be so powerful. You can make anything with it, castles in the sky, ponies, Christmas day, and yes, even friends, which, if you're anything like me, you will carry with you throughout your life.

Keep dreaming,

Nikki

Acknowledgements

First of all I must say a big thank you to my brilliant agent, Julia Churchill who gave me the golden ticket and held my hand through from slush pile to book shelves. And my fabulous editor Clare Whitston and assistant Helen Bray at OUP who patiently guided me through the next bit. But before all that happened it was the members of my writing group, Sandi, Allie, Lucy G, Lisa, Suzanna, Deborah, Eira, Phil, Becky, and Lucy S, whose encouragement, advice, wine, crisps, and friendship nourished both me and the story. And my husband, Dylan, and children Morgan, Eddie, and Harvey who gave early drafts the thumbs up, and paid for a break at Deb and Bob's Devon writing retreat so that I could finish the book in peace. And lastly to my sister who taught me to read, my brother whose imagination was inspirational, and my mum and dad who wisely acted as if it was normal for a child to talk to imaginary people.

Song lyrics on page 37-38 are from 'Dream a Little Dream of Me', by Gus Kahn.

Nikki Sheehan is the youngest daughter of a rocket scientist. She went to a convent school in Cambridge where she was taught by real nuns in long black habits.

After university Nikki's first job was subtitling the Simpsons. She then studied psychology, retrained as a journalist, and wrote features about child psychology for parenting magazines and the national press. She is married and lives in Brighton with her husband, three children, two dogs, a cat and an ever-fluctuating number of hamsters.

www.nikkisheehan.com